Antonio's new plan had revolved around courting Liliana, breaking down her resistance in stages.

And with a single "okay," she'd thrown everything out of whack. He felt like he'd been pushing with all his strength against an immovable object when suddenly all resistance was removed.

Then she'd thrown him for a loop again by whisking off his tie. As the silk had hissed as if relieved to part with his shirt, her eyes had been turbid with so many emotions. He thought he'd seen shyness, uncertainty, resignation, recklessness…and hunger.

Then, she touched him.

She slipped that small, delicate hand beneath the shirt that suddenly felt on fire and slid her burning palm over his flesh. Dipping low, as if she was searching out his heart.

* * *

Billionaire Boss, M.D.
is part of Mills & Boon Desire's
The Billionaires of Black Castle series:
Only their dark pasts could lead these men
to the light of true love.

BILLIONAIRE BOSS, M.D.

BY
OLIVIA GATES

This is a work of fiction. Names, characters, places, locations and
incidents are purely fictional and bear no relationship to any real
life individuals, living or dead, or to any actual places, business
establishments, locations, events or incidents. Any resemblance is
entirely coincidental.

First Published in Great Britain 2016
By Mills & Boon, an imprint of HarperCollins*Publishers*
1 London Bridge Street, London, SE1 9GF

© 2016 Olivia Gates

ISBN: 978-0-263-06538-1

Our policy is to use papers that are natural, renewable and recyclable
products and made from wood grown in sustainable forests. The logging
and manufacturing processes conform to the legal environmental
regulations of the country of origin.

Printed and bound in Great Britain
by CPI Antony Rowe, Chippenham, Wiltshire

USA TODAY bestselling author **Olivia Gates** has written over forty books in action/adventure, thriller, medical, paranormal and contemporary romance. Her signature is her uber-alpha male heroes. Whether they're gods, black-ops agents, virtuoso surgeons or ruthless billionaires, they all fall in love once and for life with the only women who can match them and bring them to their knees. She loves to hear from readers always, so don't hesitate to email her at oliviagates@gmail.com.

One

"Lili…look alive! The boss man himself is about to arrive."

Liliana Accardi swung away from the microscope to impale her coworker with a glare, his rhyming—whether he meant it or not—annoying her.

But it was just as well he'd interrupted her. Instead of the gray-scaled cells she was supposed to be studying, she'd been seeing only red. Ever since she'd heard the news that would end all her professional and scientific dreams. No way was she rushing off to go stand in line while said new "boss man" inspected them like a shepherd inspected his newly acquired flock.

Brian Saunders raised his hands in a "don't kill the messenger" gesture. "I just think you should come, if only to get firsthand word on the direction of his management. Maybe he'll allow you to carry on with your work, after all."

"Yeah, sure. From what I've read about him since I

started my morning with the delightful news of his take-over, Antonio Balducci rules his empire with a steel fist. He'll never allow me independence."

Brian spread his arms. "You know me, I never say never." At her hardening glare, he grinned. "I'm in the same hijacked boat as you. I just decided to deal with my captivity and go on the journey with a different attitude."

She huffed, deflating in her chair.

Brian was right. He was just another victim of the tsunami takeover. She should save her wrath for their new boss.

But Balducci wouldn't be *her* boss for long. Not if he insisted on sweeping years' worth of work and results under the rug and forcing them to dance to his profit-hungry tune.

Despite a medical degree, two master's degrees and lucrative offers, she'd spent years at Biomedical Innovation Lab with a salary that barely paid the bills. All to do marginalized but necessary research.

Until Balducci Research and Development opened its bottomless maw and swallowed them whole. They now sloshed deep in its belly among other chomped-off acquisitions.

What most galled her was the humiliating speed with which everything had been initiated and finalized. The commercialized global whale, a major tentacle of the Black Castle Enterprises leviathan, had assimilated them in mere hours.

Antonio Balducci, the billionaire celebrity surgeon, had tossed a hundred million dollars their way—chump change for him—and once again proved that money was the most powerful incentive on earth.

"Uh-oh." Brian took a step back as he spoke. "You've got that look on your face."

She frowned. "What look?"

"The one you get when you've decided to go to war."

She huffed a chuckle, half amused, half embarrassed. "I didn't realize I was *that* easy to read. After all the years I spent battling my verbal incontinence, thanks for letting me know I've only developed the mental and emotional variety."

An indulgent smile lit up Brian's genial face. "You're just straightforward and spontaneous."

She rolled her eyes. "Which are the PC words for unrestrained and blunt."

"And it's something everyone is thankful for."

She groaned. "You mean it's not only you as my best friend who can see through me? Everyone else can read me like a ten-foot neon sign?"

Brian's grin was appeasement itself. "And they love you for it. In a world full of pretense and games, you're a rarity and an incredible relief. Not to mention extremely cute."

"An outspoken five-year-old is cute. A transparent thirty-one-year-old is not."

Brian wrapped an arm around her shoulder and gave her an affectionate squeeze. "You'll be cute when you're a hundred and thirty-one." He pulled her up. "Now let's go meet our new boss. I have a feeling this won't be as bad as you think."

Taking off her lab coat, she tossed him a challenging glance. "I bet you it's worse."

"You're on." He never could resist a challenge. "If I'm right, you go on a date with one of the restless bachelors that plague my serenely married existence."

Unable to resist Brian's infectious good cheer any longer, a smile spread Lili's lips. All nine of Brian's brothers and brothers-in-law were either single or divorced. He and his wife, Darla, were always trying to set them up.

"But if I'm right," Lili said, "you strike me off your list

of possible bachelordom cures. I'm the last woman on earth
you should consider for such a task, anyway."

"I know, because you'll never get married. You've told
me a hundred times." He grinned knowingly. "All the
women who turn out to be the best wives say that. In-
cluding Darla."

Lili stifled a scoff. "You're comparing me to Darla,
the paragon of domesticity and motherhood, and a savvy
businesswoman to boot, when I can barely manage a single life that consists of work, exercise, sleep, study, rinse
and repeat?"

"Details, details." Brian winked as he held the door
open for her. "You could well be twins where it counts."

She shook her head, but let him have the last word. She
was nothing like Darla or any other woman born with the
ability to conduct intimate relationships or nurture families. Like her mother. And she'd long been at peace with
that.

So she was confident she'd win their bet, and at least
one good thing would come out of their current mess. Brian
would finally stop trying to shove her into his version of
a fulfilling existence.

As she passed him on her way out of the lab, she swept
it in one last regretful look.

If things went according to her projections, as she was
certain they would, this would be the last time she saw it.

Their new boss was late.

As she sat in her usual seat halfway down the conference table, Lili fumed.

Either Balducci had met his demise—and they couldn't
possibly be that lucky—or he didn't consider them worthy
of his legendary punctuality. And that boded even worse
for them than she'd expected.

Her bleary gaze scanned the room. All thirty of the BIL

OLIVIA GATES 11

employees were there and unlike her, they'd all clearly run
back home to dress for the occasion, leaving only her in
an appropriately drab-as-her-mood outfit. Also unlike her,
they seemed relieved, even excited at the takeover. Even
hating this as much as she did, Lili realized why. She had
been feeling the toll of the obstacles they'd had to tackle
continuously to do what other better-funded labs did in a
fraction of the time. But to her, setbacks, false starts and
near misses were an expected part of scientific endeavor.
It seemed her attitude hadn't been shared by the others
as she'd thought, and she was the only one with a purely
negative stance on the takeover. And a hostile one toward
the man behind it.

Everyone else was awed by the very mention of the legendary Dr. Antonio Balducci. The buzz she was sensing
wasn't only over any favorable expectations with him at the
helm, but also over the opportunity of meeting him in the
flesh. The ladies especially looked aflutter at the prospect.
From her online research of him, she grudgingly conceded
their reaction was the normal one, not hers.

Since she reserved her curiosity for scientific matters,
she'd barely known a thing about him before she'd heard
the news. After she had, she'd gone through the stages of
shock, denial and fury, and through everything she could
find on him on the net.

To her surprise, she found three parallels with him from
the first thing she read. Like her, he was a doctor, and he'd
been born to an Italian father and was an only child. But
that was where their similarities ended.

He was an American now, naturalized three years ago,
while she was an American through her mother. Both his
parents were long dead, while her own mother had died
only a year ago, and her father who had never existed in
her life, had recently—and to her continuing surprise, very
enthusiastically—reentered it.

Pulling her thoughts away from that development, she turned them to the man at hand.

Not much was known about Antonio Balducci's early life. He was raised in Austria, his mother's homeland, where he became fluent in six languages and where he lived until he graduated from medical school. It was only about eight years ago that information about him, staggering in quantity and quality, had started pouring in.

That was when he'd shot onto the world scene, an awe-inspiring figure whose success in every field he entered was phenomenal. Being a founding member of the global juggernaut Black Castle Enterprises was meticulously documented, as well as his founding of the conglomerate's medical R & D business—the arm of his empire that had taken over her beloved lab.

Adding to his lure for the media was his effect on the females of the species. Women went nuts over him like they did over music and soccer legends like Presley and Beckham. If she'd thought his effect a media exaggeration, she was seeing empirical evidence of his irresistibility to women right before her eyes. And that was before he actually arrived.

But all that wasn't what he was best known for. Most of his fame stemmed from being sought after by the world's elite to perform or even consult on their rejuvenations. But his *biggest* achievement was being hailed as a trauma and reconstructive surgical god whose work bordered on magic.

She ground her teeth together. The only magic she thought Balducci practiced was the black kind. To her, he was the capricious force who was pulverizing everything she'd worked for, just because he could.

And the damned man dared be late for her destruction!

Suddenly conversation was cut off as if someone had

hit Stop. She looked up and saw all eyes glued to the doorway behind her. That meant...

She swung around to catch the moment when the man who'd quashed her ambitions bulldozed into her territory. And it was her turn to feel she'd been caught in a stasis field.

As everything decelerated to a standstill, a mental protest went off inside her mind.

No one should be all that, and look like that, too. Is there no fairness in this world?

Gaping and unable to do anything about it, she stared at the figure in the doorway. In a slate-gray suit that molded to a body that belonged to a world-class athlete, not a surgeon and entrepreneur, Antonio Balducci dwarfed the room with his physical and personal presence.

While viewing his photos online, she'd dismissed the possibility that he looked that good in real life, believing he'd had his photos touched up or he'd achieved his perfection surgically.

But even across a packed room, she knew neither of that was true. If anything, the photos had downplayed his looks. And she could discern surgical interventions from a mile away and she had no doubt whatsoever that every one of Antonio Balducci's jaw-dropping assets was authentic.

At forty, the man had skin that looked like an alloy of polished copper and bronze. The tensile medium was pulled tight over a masterpiece of bone structure. Her fingers itched to indulge in a much-neglected pastime and sketch its every detail: the leonine forehead, the patrician nose, the slashing cheekbones, the powerful jaw and cleft chin.

After transferring the framework of his unique face to paper, she'd linger over every hair framing his majestic head, the most robust mass of raven silk she'd ever seen. But among all those wonders, two things transfixed her.

The wide, sculpted lips bowed in a mysterious quirk. And his eyes.

Apart from their amazing shape and startling blueness, it was what they conveyed that sent her heartbeat into disarray. Contrary to the opacity of his smile, his gaze radiated an amalgam of expressions. Amusement and austerity. Curiosity and superiority. Astuteness and calculation. And a dozen other things she couldn't decide on.

Those were the eyes of a scientist. But equally they were the eyes of a conqueror.

Which probably summed him up just right.

As he walked into room, déjà vu struck her.

Among his photos, one in particular had arrested her. A rare shot of him and his partners in Black Castle Enterprises.

They'd been captured as they'd exited their opulent New York headquarters en masse. It was an unrehearsed shot that was far more hard-hitting than any posed shot could have been, and it had earned its photographer instant fame.

The photo had captured their essence in such starkness that when it was published, Black Castle stock prices spiked to unheard-of levels. The men looked like a pantheon of warrior gods who'd descended to earth in the guise of ultramodern businessmen. The array of sheer male power and beauty in that photo was breathtaking. It had clearly robbed the whole world of breath.

Yet even among those gods among men, Antonio had stood out.

Not only had his brand of gorgeousness thrummed the chords of her specific taste, something else had fascinated her on a fundamental level. Though they were all extraordinary, she'd felt he had an edge over the other men. Even in the remoteness of a photo she felt he had the coolest head, the most deliberate mind. Even in her fury, that had appealed to her so fiercely she'd found herself saving the photo for leisurely inspection at a later date, maybe even as material for a future illustration.

And here he was in the impossibly perfect flesh, the epitome of splendor and sangfroid.

She wouldn't be surprised if he belonged to some next-step-in-evolution elite who'd eliminated all human frailties and imperfections and who operated on pure, merciless intellect.

He now stopped at the table and leaned his six-foot-plus frame to flatten his palms on its shining surface.

Seething with renewed resentment at his effect on her, she followed his serene gaze as it swept the room. From the chain reaction she felt going off around her, he seemed to be making eye contact with everyone. Everyone but her. His gaze skipped over her as if she were a blank space.

After the momentary consternation of being passed over, she was relieved. If his mere presence provoked those reactions in her, she didn't want to find out what she'd feel if that all-seeing gaze bored into her.

Once he'd had them holding their breath, he inclined his head. "Thanks for accommodating me at such short notice. I'm glad you could all make it."

Man, that voice. If everything about him weren't too much already, that darkest vocal spell would have been bad enough on its own. Making it even worse was an ephemeral accent that intertwined through its meticulous articulation, deepening its impact.

As murmured responses rustled around the room, he straightened to his towering height.

"I don't want to hold you up, especially those of you whose schedule is nine to five, so I'll get right to the point of my visit." A perfectly timed dramatic pause. "I hope you're as optimistic as I am about the new state of affairs, and will find working under the Balducci umbrella a rewarding experience, scientifically and financially."

He spread a prompting smile around the room and Lili saw everyone grin back at him like hypnotized fools.

Without taking his eyes off the assembly, he gestured to someone she realized had been behind him all along. The shorter man in turn directed four people behind him to come forward. They had piles of folders, which they passed around the room. When it was her turn to receive one, she stared down at the inch-thick glossy volume graced with Balducci's distinctive serpent logo.

"In your hands is comprehensive info on Balducci's operations," he explained. "As well as the mission statement for its new merger with your facility." Merger, huh? Big of him to call his incursion that. "Until you read everything in detail, let me give you a brief summation.

"I founded Balducci R & D to furnish the world with visionary medical solutions. A dynamic, adventurous and fast-paced researching, manufacturing and distribution organization specializing in state-of-the-art products and technologies in a number of leading medical fields. My aim remains to provide the medical community with unparalleled clinical products that set the trend in medicine. For six years, Balducci has been the primary supplier, to hospitals, clinics and research institutions, of advanced medical solutions in a variety of fields. With a constantly growing global team of the best the world has to offer in their disciplines, which I'm proud for you to be a part of now, we provide exceptional value, service and support much above the industry standard. And we achieve the highest customer retention rates in every market we currently dominate. But there are new frontiers I aim to conquer." Yeah, just what she'd figured. "And this is where you come in."

Everyone sat up, taking even closer notice. The man really had masterful timing and delivery.

When he'd made sure everyone was hanging on his

every breath, he went on, "I don't need to tell you that your team is composed of some of the most avant-garde researchers of our time. I have no doubt you're well aware of your individual and collective worth. I certainly am best equipped to know it. I'm still suffering from the very sizable hole in my assets it took to acquire your services."

As chuckles of pleasure spread through the room, Lili's hackles rose higher. What was wrong with her colleagues? They were proud they had a price? Sure, he pretended "acquiring their services" had taken a toll on him, but they all knew this was untrue. The man was worth over a dozen *billion* dollars!

Then he spoke again, dousing her new spurt of irritation.

"The methods and results you've contributed to the medical community working with limited funding and resources is nothing short of astounding. Each and every one of you is exactly the kind of unique-approach, enterprising scientist that Balducci covets. As you'll see from the documents you have in your possession now, each of you has been assigned to a project I believe you're most suited for, where you'll have anything you could possibly want to make progress in it, and hopefully reach a breakthrough. And let me be clear. By anything, I do mean *anything*. My assistants will be available to provide any of your needs. But my own door is always open if what you need is too ambitious, as I hope all your work with me will be."

By the time he finished, she was gaping again.

The man was overpowering. Velvet over steel over an enigma. Not only the most magnificent male she'd ever seen, but the most persuasive, too.

What he'd outlined was every scientist's fairy tale come true. Unlimited resources to be as adventurous as they wished, caring only about the work, while funding and feasibility were being taken care of by dedicated experts with access to bottomless pockets and powered by limitless ambition. His.

He'd almost convinced even her. Almost.

But if she had to fight his hypnosis with all she had, she had no doubt the others were already in his thrall. A darting glance noted the glassy eyes of those who no longer questioned that his decreed path was the one to tread. Even Brian had a budding hero-worship expression on his face.

"That would all be well and good, *if* you were offering to fund our projects, not yours."

It wasn't until everyone swung to gape at her as if she'd thrown a grenade on the table that she realized she'd spoken.

And she did it again, without intending to.

"In your R & D career, you've consistently ignored basic research, what has produced centuries of history-changing breakthroughs, spawned whole industries and disciplines in medicine. You've also ignored the kind of research we do, of untrendy ailments that don't provoke public or market interest. You've overlooked necessary research for a jumble of popular, feel-good, cash-cow fields like the cosmetic and weight-loss industries."

The elusive smile that had been hovering on his lips suddenly froze.

All her blood followed suit.

Her heart thudding, she wished for some cosmic rewind button so she could erase what she'd just said.

Why had she spoken at all? She'd already found out her worst-case scenario would come to pass and they'd be herded wherever he wished. She didn't do posturing confrontations. She knew her power, or rather, lack thereof. So why hadn't she kept her big mouth shut and just tendered her resignation in silence?

Before she could draw another breath into her constricted lungs, he turned his head in her direction and impaled her on the lasers he had for eyes.

And all she could think was...uh-oh.

Two

Lili's heart plummeted as the world emptied of everything but this overwhelming entity who had her in his crosshairs.

Before she obeyed the flight mechanisms that screamed for her to run, tossing a "Don't bother firing me, I quit" over her shoulder, Antonio Balducci started talking, pinning her down even more.

"As my reconstructive surgeries do incorporate an aesthetic element, I do invest in the development and manufacture of all aesthetic disciplines and products."

His voice. That perfectly modulated melody of cultured lethality. A glacial sound of hair-raising beauty. Pouring all over her like a freezing/searing deluge.

Oh, crap. She hadn't thought this through. Hadn't thought at all. That bitter outburst had just...well, burst out of her. What if he got verbally combative?

She'd flay him right back, that was what. Before she ran.

But before she snatched the next breath, still transfixing her with that impossibly blue stare, he went on, serene and far more menacing because of it, "As you'll see from the info I provided, only twenty percent of my operations focus on the 'popular, feel-good, cash-cow' side of my specialty."

Whoa. He was quoting what she'd said. When she'd thought he'd only realized she'd been talking—and criticizing him openly—just before her tirade ended.

But he hadn't only heard her, he'd memorized what she'd said. He'd even *sounded* like her when he'd quoted her. She had a feeling he could recite everything she'd said word for word. Which shouldn't surprise her. It only substantiated her theory of him being some sort of post–human being.

His eyes bored into her, making her feel he'd drilled a hole into her skull and was probing her brain. "The remaining eighty percent of my operations revolve around the more relevant sides of my field of interest, and those of others. Problem is those don't generate media coverage or capture the market's imagination. This is just the state of the world. I didn't invent it."

"No, you just exploit it."

At her volley, he tilted his head, as if plunging deeper into her mind. Then those chiseled lips twitched and her stuttering heart burst into a stumbling gallop.

"The pursuit of luxury products tends to trump necessary ones and 'cash cows' are such for a reason. Alas, human beings will be human beings. I assure you, I have no role in their condition. So what would you have me do? Not provide them with what they wish for? Judge their foibles and let someone else reap the benefits of catering to them? Benefits I eventually put to uses you might deem to approve of?"

Was he teasing her? Nah. He couldn't be.

"And aesthetic concerns are not frivolous luxuries. No matter how *you* view them, they do greatly affect people's psychological and mental health. I don't morally grade what people need or consider worth paying for. Who's to say that products that reverse the signs of aging aren't as important to a substantial percentage of people as depression treatment? And would you view me and my business any kinder if you knew I also research the latter? And am involved in actual aging reversal research, too?"

Okay, he *was* teasing her. Poking fun at her, more like, making her criticism sound misinformed and holier-than-thou, or at the very least naive. And seeming to draw appreciation from everyone in the room while at it, adding to the unhealthy awe he'd already garnered.

He only made her feel like a hedgehog with its bristles standing on end. Mostly because she found her own lips twitching, too.

So, the man had a sense of humor. Had he come complete with it, or had he had it grafted as another weapon in his overflowing arsenal? Or did he realize the benefits of manipulating lesser beings with the illusion of ease and indulgence, and had a subroutine written into his program that he could activate at will?

"Among the commendable-by-your-standards investments I can afford to make with the profits of not-so-commendable ones, there are ones in my own field. Restoring functionality, for instance. Thanks to the money-generating machines, I can invest heavily into integrated prosthetics, microsurgery appliances and research, scar prevention and treatment, and lately, muscle and nerve tissue regeneration. *That* endeavor will be the main focus of this facility in our collaboration. I'm not even putting a limit to the budget for this one. Whatever it takes to reach a breakthrough, I'll provide the resources."

Then just as he'd given her his undiluted attention, he took it away, making her feel as if he'd taken the chair and the ground beneath it right out from under her.

Before she realized she had a response to his rebuttal, she found herself sitting up, her pose confrontational, her tone even more challenging. "Well, it's all quite laudable, I'm sure, that—while not advancing basic science as only someone of your clout and resources can—you invest in advancing your field. But 'this facility' already has its own array of 'commendable' projects under way, and it would be a loss that can't be measured in money if we shelved them to head in the direction where you point us. Just because you acquired our services doesn't mean you can cancel all our efforts, or should dictate which break-through is worth benefiting from our expertise backed by your unlimited funds and clout."

This time everyone in the room turned to stab her on the pointy edge of their disapproval. The canny man had already won them over to his side, promising them shiny new projects, not to mention endless means to frolic in the land of scientific possibilities to their hearts' content.

This time, Balducci didn't give her the courtesy of a re-sponse. His argument had been designed to win her over, or at least chastise her. From her renewed attack he must have decided further response wouldn't make a difference. As the epitome of pragmatism someone of his success must be, he'd decided she wasn't worth the extra effort. He wouldn't waste more time on a dissenting cog now that he was certain he had the rest of the machine wagging its components awaiting his directives.

Turning his attention to the rest, he directed everyone to read the folder carefully. Everyone's roles and projects for the next year were spelled out to the last detail. Tomor-row would be the first working day under the new man-agement, and he would be available at the provided email or phone number for any questions, concerns or minor ad-justments. Any major suggestions would be discussed in the next general meeting. He closed by thanking everyone in such a way as to have them swooning all over again before he dismissed the assembly.

Everyone rose to shuffle around him, waiting their turn to catch his eye or shake his hand. Lili cursed them for the limpets they'd turned into, and cursed him for turning them into such. Still, she was thankful for the milling crowd that gave her the cover under which to escape. Snatching her bag up, leaving the folder behind, she rose. Head down, giving him the widest berth she could, she made a beeline for the door. To her dismay, he was making short work of everyone, and those he'd dismissed were already squeezing out of the room, hindering her escape. She barely curbed the urge to push through them and forced herself to take her turn walking out. Still she bristled at the censure and pity in their oblique gazes, but mostly at *his* disconcerting vibe at her back.

In minutes, she burst out into LA's summer afternoon. She usually hated the transition from the beloved seclusion of her lab and the building's controlled climate to the hot, humid bustle of the sprawling city. But now she was relieved to be out of what had become a place she'd hate to set foot in again. The place that was now Antonio Balducci's.

She'd reached her Mazda in the parking lot when she felt as if an arrow had lodged between her shoulder blades.

It was his voice. Calling her.

What the hell!

Though her hand froze in midair with the remote, her thoughts streaked ahead. Did she dread him so much, like a kid dreads the headmaster singling her out, that she was imagining it? Even if he had called her, he must be here only to get his car, too.

In the next millisecond her analytical mind negated that theory. Antonio Balducci wouldn't use public parking. He wouldn't have driven himself here in the first place.

One of those people who followed in his wake like efficient phantoms must be his chauffeur. He couldn't have just stumbled on her. Which meant he must have pursued her specifically, and very quickly. Which made even less sense than any other theory.

As her mind burned rubber, his voice carried to her on the warm, moist breeze again, the very sound of forbearance.

"Dr. Accardi, I'd appreciate a word."

She swung around, her face scrunching against the declining sun in a scowl. "What for?"

She groaned at how petulant and aggressive she sounded. But this guy tripped all her wires. Watching him approach her like a sleek panther sent them haywire. He was so big he made the parking lot claustrophobic, so unhurried he made her feel cornered, so unearthly gorgeous he made her every nerve ache.

When he stopped two feet away, he siphoned the air from the world. Harsh sunlight struck deepest blue and indigo off his raven hair—which she realized had a smattering of silver at the temples—and threw his every feature in sharp relief, intensifying his beauty. She was sure she looked horrible in such unforgiving lighting, but Dr. Paragon here? He was even more perfect at such total exposure.

As the word *exposure* dragged her mind places it didn't want to go, she yanked it back and squinted way up at him even from her five-foot-eight height. She mentally kicked herself for not having her sunglasses as a barrier to hide behind, as protection against his all-seeing gaze. But since she always went home long after sundown, frequently not at all, she rarely packed them. As if they would have been an extra burden in her mobile home of a tote bag. But that was what she was—always ready for all possibilities in her work, and the personification of unpreparedness in her personal life. Which she now was in such a close encounter with the monolith before her.

Just as she thought he'd stare down at her until he melted her at his feet, he raised his hand, making her notice the folder he'd been holding all the time.

"I brought you this," he said. "You must have forgotten it."

He followed her to give her the folder she'd left behind?

Her mind raced to decipher him and his actions as her senses crackled with his nearness. When she spoke, she sounded exasperated, even if she was more so with herself. "No, I haven't forgotten it."

"So you left it on purpose."

"Apart from omission or commission, are there any other reasons I could have left it behind?"

One corner of his lips lifted in acknowledgment of her chastising logic, intensifying his already staggering effect. She hated to think how he'd look outright smiling or laughing.

"My apologies for the redundant comment. Will asking about the reason you did leave it meet with the same exasperation?"

She exhaled, trying to find the civil, easygoing person inside her who was generally in the driver's seat... and failing. "From what I read about you, and from the evidence of your achievements and power, you possess an unchartable IQ. I'm sure you need none of it to work out the reason I did."

"Indeed. Your motivation is quite clear. It was a material rejection to underscore your verbal one. I had just hoped it was a simple oversight on your part."

"And since you now know it wasn't, if this will be all..."

His forward movement cut off her backward one, along with her air supply again. "Actually, it won't be all. Bringing you the folder was incidental to the main reason I sought you out." He employed another of those pauses he used like weapons, making her bate whatever breath was left in her lungs. "I'd like to further discuss your objections to my policies."

She gaped up at him. That was the last thing she would have thought he'd say, or want. Not that she could actually think with him so near. She could only react.

Not finding any appropriate reaction, the first thing that surfaced in her mind was another accusation. "You said you didn't want to hold us up."

He gave a conceding tilt of his head that made his hair rearrange itself into another pattern of perfection. She could swear she heard the silk swish and sigh.

"I did make it clear I meant those who have a nine-to-five schedule. You're not one of those. In fact, you're the only one who almost makes this place your home."

She stared into his spellbinding eyes as he stared back with the same intentness.

How did he know that?

How? Because the man had a level of intelligence and efficiency she'd never before encountered. It stood to reason he'd researched the staff before he'd acquired them. Though she'd thought they'd be too insignificant for him individually, she had to revise that opinion. To reach his level of success he couldn't be a detached leader who left details to others. He had to be hands-on. Nothing and no one was too trivial or below his notice.

She wouldn't be surprised if he had invasive info on everyone who held or would hold any position in his businesses…and had memorized it, too. Thinking that disconcerted her on a primal level. Even if there wasn't much about her to know, just that he did know it put her at an even bigger disadvantage, if that was even possible.

"Nothing to go back home to?"

His quiet question surprised an unfiltered answer from her. "There never really was."

Her dismay deepened at the contemplative cast that came over his gaze. She'd exposed herself even more, and she held him accountable for it, him with his damned hypnotic power.

But her consternation was swept away by the surge of memories. Memories of growing up with only her mother, who moved her around so much following her medical career she'd never stayed long enough in one place to form real friendships. Only when Lili had entered medical school herself had her mother finally settled in LA, just before she fell prey to early-onset Alzheimer's. Lili had gone back to live with her, before being forced to put her in a home for four years before her death a year ago. Her mother's house remained a place to crash when she wasn't working. Being a workaholic was what saved her from feeling lonely. It was the only other thing she'd inherited from her mother. Hopefully. Home had always been wherever she worked. This lab had been her home for the past three years. Her haven. Until *he* happened.

"There you go again."

"There I go what again?"

His lips spread wider. The ground beneath her tilted. "Using me as target practice for your poison-laced glances."

Choking on the heart that his smile yanked into her throat, she shrugged. "They're just dipped in heavy tranquilizers. Or loaded with fifty thousand volts."

At that, he did something she'd dreaded in theory, but had thought would never come to pass in reality. Not in her presence.

He threw his head back and laughed.

And his laughter was...horrible. It did terrible things

to her insides, had her hormones rushing in torrents in her system.

Great. Just great. Just when she discovered she had those kinds of hormones after all, they had to be activated by him of all men. And in broad daylight. When he was laughing his magnificent head off at her, no less.

To make things worse, one big, elegant hand rose to wipe his left cheek. He'd laughed so hard, it had wrung a tear from his eye. Fantastic.

But what was really worth marveling at was how moisture smeared his hewn flesh. Her thoughts caught fire imagining him drenched in exertion, during or after he'd—

Shaking away the sensual images only lodged them deeper into her brain. Her tongue tingled with until-now unknown urges—the sudden longing to drag him down to her, so she could trace that cheekbone, taste his virility. Only his hand combing back the hair that had fallen over his forehead distracted her from those idiotic impulses. The hand of the virtuoso surgeon he was, powerful, grace-ful, skillful…in every possible way, no doubt—

For God's sake, stop. *Stop noticing his every detail and getting arrhythmia over each one!*

But in the absence of others, she had no buffer against his sheer charisma and sensual power—both of which she was certain he didn't even mean to exercise on her. A man like him must have them on all the time on auto. She'd never even thought men like him existed outside of leg-ends and fairy tales.

After she'd become a jumbled mess, he sobered, the wattage of his smile dazzling her.

"So you don't want me dead, just incapacitated."

She fidgeted, her tote getting heavier by the second. "Ideally, long enough to remove you from my path. I want you gone from my world, not the one at large."

"That's big of you."

Nerves jangling at the outright teasing she could no longer mistake, she sighed. "When it doesn't come to my lab—yours now—I do recognize that, even if it's to your humongous advantage, you are a formidable force for good."

His eyebrows shot up. "Considering your views of me back there it's unexpected to hear you admit that."

"I'm a surprise a second. To myself most of all today. I sure didn't mean to say any of the things I said back there."

"So you didn't mean them?"

"I said I didn't mean to *say* them."

"So you did mean them."

"Can't mean anything more, in the context of my own concerns." She shot him a defiant glance, this man who'd detained her because he could do anything he wanted and have the world bend over backward to accommodate him. "You're sadly misguided if you think you'll get an apology or a retraction."

"You've given me both when you deigned to recognize my worth to the world."

"Still doesn't change the fact that I wish I had the power to make you disappear."

He shook his head, his grin widening, wreaking more havoc with her already compromised nerves.

"What do you find so funny now?" she mumbled sullenly.

"Not funny, delightful. You're definitely not the first person to wish to eliminate me, but you're the first to tell me so to my face."

"Hey, watch your terminology. You go around using words like *poison-laced* and *eliminate*, and if something ever befalls you, I'm a prime suspect. I only wish to be rid of your disruption. All I want is to go back to work tomorrow to the news that you've withdrawn your bid and let us be."

"And if a way presented itself for you to make this happen?"

"I wouldn't hesitate."

He gave another chuckle. "It doesn't seem you were handed discretion at the cosmic assembly line. Are you this blunt with everyone?"

Noticing the watchfulness that entered his gaze at this question, getting the feeling that he somehow didn't relish the idea, she shrugged a shoulder. "Not since I was a kid. Or at least I thought so, until just before you arrived and Brian told me I'm transparent. I thought it was only my expressions that everyone could read, that I wasn't as incontinent verbally, then you started your hypnotic session and I felt my colleagues being assimilated into your hive mind, and I...well, any tact I thought I cultivated evaporated."

"You don't like this about yourself." It was a statement, not a question. "You should. In fact, you should continue being as outspoken about the grievance you have with me. I have a feeling it goes beyond objecting to the change in course I'm proposing."

She almost snorted. "Proposing? You mean dictating. And you think that's not enough for me to consider you and your takeover the worst thing that could happen to this place?"

"I didn't get the impression anyone else shared that unfavorable opinion."

This time, she did snort. "Of course, you didn't. You must be surprised there was even one dissenting voice." Her blood frothed again at how her colleagues had succumbed to him without even a fight. "You know very well the effect you have on people."

"I only noticed the inflammatory one I had on you."

"Yeah, well, I guess I'm the mad scientist type."

"Aren't you all supposed to be that?"

She exhaled. "I thought so. But the promise of open-ended coddling proved irresistible to my colleagues."

"But not to you."

Her shoulders hunched with futility. "Yeah."

The blue of his eyes seemed to intensify. "Why? What makes you so resistant? Why is the promise of everything you've ever dreamed of at your fingertips not as alluring to you?"

"I told you why in agonizing detail and you already know I hate redundancy. Especially after you took such pleasure in deconstructing my argument and having the last word."

"I don't remember I had the last word."

"You didn't bother to have it. You just ignored mine."

"I chose not to engage you again in front of everyone, decided to do so in private. As I am doing now."

"You shouldn't have. I have nothing more to say."

"So do you only take exception to leaving your own project behind?"

"I take exception to being forced to."

"Your results won't evaporate if you shelve them for a while."

"I see no reason to while I'm making progress."

"There are many reasons, scientific and financial. You'll also gain expertise working on my projects, your own work would eventually benefit."

"If you think I need expertise you shouldn't want me working on your projects."

"I meant added expertise. I wouldn't have paid all that money if I thought you were anything but the best."

She waved his placating response away. "You didn't pay anything for me. That hundred million—"

"*Two* hundred million. Half of which is funding for phase one of all the projects I have planned for you."

She forced her open mouth closed. "What's a hundred million dollars more, huh? But whatever you paid was for our collective services and obedience, probably for the rest of our lives. Now that you've found one troublemaking apple in your bushel, you can always toss it out."

"I have no intention of tossing you out."

"Well, I intend to jump out of the cart myself."

His eyes narrowed. "You're contemplating quitting?"

"I'm done contemplating."

His expression went blank. But though there was nothing to read in it anymore, she felt she was getting the first real glimpse of what he hid beneath the polished exterior of the genius surgeon and suave businessman. Something lurked below his placid surface, something more sharp-edged than his state-of-the-art scalpels. *Someone* utterly ruthless. No, more. Someone lethal.

Which was stupid. Whatever else he was, this man was a healer. He didn't end lives, he saved them. All these feverish thoughts must be the sun frying her brain. Or was it such intense and close exposure to him?

Then he spoke again, sending her every hair standing on end. "It's clear contemplation has nothing to do with your decision. I wouldn't even call such a knee-jerk reaction one."

He again sounded like when he'd been addressing their assembly, making her realize how deliberate and calculated he had been in comparison to how he'd been talking to her now. He had been out to subdue and mesmerize everyone. He was trying to make her bow to his will now.

Well, he should have realized by now that his tried and true methods only backfired with her.

Bent on walking away this time, she stood as tall as she could. "Call it what you like. I quit, Dr. Balducci. I'm sure my loss will be nothing more than a negligible annoyance, since BIL is chock-full of those who will ecstatically do your bidding."

"You can't quit, Dr. Accardi."

"Because the lump sum you paid included my price? Just a sec..." She took the bag off her shoulder, rummaged for her wallet, pulled the money she found and stuck the bills out to him.

"What's that supposed to be?"

Extending her hand as close as she dared get to him, she met his glowering with her own. "I don't know what the going rate per head was, but taking into account the premises and everything else, I'm sure I didn't cost you more than that."

His eyes fell to the notes before he raised them to her, full of mockery. "I assure you, you cost me much more than that."

She refused to lower her hand. "You let me know exactly what I cost you, and I'll pay for my freedom in installments. Consider this the first one."

As he realized she wasn't joking, his gaze clashed with hers as if to make her cower before him. She was sure such a glare had brought many adversaries to their knees. Tough, it was going to let him down this time. Even if she felt he'd set her on fire if she held his stare any longer.

A second before she averted her own eyes, he suddenly looked down at the money. He plucked three hundred-dollar bills from the bunch before he raised his eyes again and almost knocked her flat on her back with the mischief filling them.

"Now you really can't quit."

She gaped at his wicked grin. "What?"

"You just paid me for shares in your facility. Now you have to stay and run the place with me. Or for me."

Before another thought could fire in her stalled brain, he turned and strode away.

Out of nowhere, a sleek black limo slithered soundlessly up to him.

Before he got in, he turned to her with a mock salute and said, "See you tomorrow, partner."

Three

Antonio caught himself grinning again and again all the way back to his mansion in Holmby Hills.

Shaking his head for the umpteenth time since he'd left Liliana Accardi gaping at him as if he'd grown a spiked tail and leather wings and taken flight, he again wondered what the hell had happened in that parking lot. Actually, what the hell had happened since she'd blasted him in that meeting room.

This wasn't what he'd envisioned at all. Not after everything had gone according to plan. At first.

He'd made the bid on the lab, knowing he'd find no resistance. He'd finalized everything in record time before moving to the next phase—conquering his new subordinates. He'd done that, too, with more acceptance than his best projections, thanks to his long-perfected methods of making people do his bidding.

He'd started practicing his influence from childhood when he'd been in the clutches of The Organization, which had taken him and hundreds of children to turn them into lethal mercenaries. Even among his brotherhood, as unyielding as they were, he'd enjoyed a unique position of power. While Phantom—Numair now—had been the leader everyone deferred to, it had been Antonio everyone trusted to have the most levelheaded opinion. When he'd become their medical expert, they'd trusted him with their very lives.

He'd taken that skill into the outside world after they'd escaped The Organization. Normal people had been no match for the sway he'd honed with some of the world's most shrewd and lethal people. He'd plowed through the worlds of medicine and business like a laser, being described by rivals and allies alike as irresistible and unstoppable. Not that he reached his goals through aggression or intimidation. He relied on persuasion and manipulation, so no one had a reason to fight him and every reason to succumb to him.

Among his brothers, he was the one who had an equally close and friction-free relationship with all. Yet he'd allowed not even them beyond the serene facade he'd refined.

They believed it was Wildcard—or Ivan Konstantinov as he now called himself—who knew Antonio fully, as he'd been closest to him since childhood. But Antonio hadn't even let Ivan in on everything he'd been through or everything he was. He hadn't told Ivan anything he was doing or planning now.

While the others had searched for their families, sought reunion with them and/or revenge on those who'd stolen them away, Ivan, who'd come to The Organization old enough to know his family, had elected not to contact his family once he'd been out. Antonio had elected not to bother with either finding his origins or seeking revenge. Or so he'd told his brothers. In reality, he'd found out everything about his family.

What he'd learned had made him think The Organization had done him a favor by abducting him. His Italian aristocracy family put its members through hell for appearances' sake, which they enforced at any expense, even abandoning or destroying any of them who threatened their traditions and standing.

As they had him.

His mother's pregnancy when she was seventeen had threatened their image. Her inappropriate lover had been dealt with, while she'd been taken away to avoid the scandal. The same day she'd given birth to him, he'd been given to an orphanage, from which he'd been culled by The Organization less than four years later. Up until that day he'd lived hoping his "real family" would find him.

It turned out he'd been better off with The Organization than in the Accardis' sterile, cold-blooded environment where relationships were warped and members turned into shells of human beings. At least The Organization had let him pursue his true inclinations, what had made him who he was. It had been there he'd forged stronger-than-blood ties with his brothers, nothing like the pathological ones his family shared.

He'd at first decided to ignore the existence of the family that had wronged him so irretrievably. But after three of his brothers had found their roots and reunited with their own families, he'd begun to feel restless until he'd realized that he was being eaten alive with the need to even the score.

And to do that, he had to destroy the Accardis. Starting with his mother.

Agreeing to or at least accepting her family's crime, she hadn't attempted to search for him, had moved on instead and gotten married three times. She'd had legitimate offspring with each of her husbands as well as adopted children. The oldest was a man five years younger than him, the youngest a girl of twelve, making his crop of half siblings no less than six.

He'd planned to infiltrate the family anonymously, to exact up close and personal retribution on those who'd had a hand in his abandonment.

But the elitist snobs hadn't opened up to him, not even with the bait of vital financial relief. Getting close to this family could be through the only way they allowed.

Through blood. Through a member.

After a thorough analysis of the extended family, he'd zeroed in on one member. Liliana Accardi.

Liliana was the daughter of Alberto Accardi, his mother's third cousin. Her American mother had escaped Italy and the poisonous Accardi family when Liliana was only one and run back to the States. But after her mother's death last year, the only child, family-less Liliana had started to reestablish relations with her father. The man who hadn't bothered to see his daughter after he'd granted her mother a lucrative divorce was now eager to welcome her into his life. Surprisingly, the rest of the Accardis seemed as enthusiastic to invite her into the family. That had added to her potential use to Antonio.

Being a fellow doctor was another thing that had made her his best choice. And the fact that she'd graduated at the top of her class, but had ended up in a minor nonprofit lab battling impossible odds. Her quixotic tendencies had only made him consider her an even easier target. Everything else about her from looks to personal history had made her the most surefire as well as most tolerable vehicle for his needs.

He'd decided to approach her in a professional setting, bait her, snare her, then through her, enter the family, exact punishment from within, then walk away when they'd all paid, each to the exact measure he'd decide they deserved.

As for Liliana, she'd been wronged, too, if on an infinitely smaller scale. Though he'd despised her for seeking the family who'd driven her mother away and made Liliana grow up alone, to court their favor and inclusion, he'd intended to be lenient with her. *If* she provided him with a smooth ride to his life's most anticipated surgery, that of excising the petrified heart of the family who'd thrown him away like so much garbage.

He'd had no doubt she'd fall at his feet like all subordinates, like all women. The plan was simple. He'd make a proposal she'd grab at. After all, it would make a much more convincing entry into her family if she was delirious at her phenomenal luck. Then when he broke it off, if she'd benefited him—and if she didn't turn out to be another soulless Accardi or a greedy female—he'd compensate her handsomely.

Then he'd entered that meeting room, delivered his opening speech, and though he'd had the expected deference and delight from everyone else, he'd gotten none of the usual fluttering anticipation and adulation from her. Instead, she'd left him in no doubt of her reaction to his takeover, nor of her opinion of him.

From then on, everything had gone off the rails.

After his first surprise at her impassioned attack on his methods, history and person, he'd tried to overpower her, herd her back to his scripted pathway. Just as he'd thought he'd put her in the place where he needed her to stay, she'd retaliated with a more incontrovertible accusation.

Everything in him had surged to engage her full-on. But that would have been fodder for gossip and would have put him in a defensive position—something he'd never let himself be in. That had been when he'd realized he'd miscalculated.

The woman he'd thought would fall into his palm like a ripe plum had turned out to be a prickly pear.

A change of strategy had been in order.

But for the first time in memory, he couldn't come up with a course of action but to dismiss her. So he'd let her final words hang there in the conference room without a rebuttal from him. That confrontation had ended with the score of Liliana Accardi one, him nothing.

He had decided to resume her conquest the next day, after he'd upgraded his plan. But he'd itched with impatience, all his senses trained on her, the only one of the staff to avoid him. He'd pretended he hadn't noticed her as she'd kept her distance on her way out, when in truth he'd noticed nothing but her.

At one point, when she'd been closest to him, his resolve to ignore her had almost broken down. But he'd managed to let her walk out without doing something stupid.

Then he'd noticed the folder.

He'd realized adjusting his plan might be for nothing. This contrary woman might not be giving him another day. She'd forced him to pursue her there and then.

He'd still been certain that once he had her one-on-one, he'd bring her back in line. But the more he'd tried, the more she'd forced him to improvise, and the more he had, the further away from his desired results he'd gotten.

Not only hadn't he managed to overwhelm her, she'd taken him by surprise again and again. He'd found himself reacting without the least premeditation, something he never did. Then he'd found himself guffawing like a fool. He hadn't meant to laugh, but her unfiltered responses had been so unexpected and droll, she'd been the one to overpower his control and intent.

Not that his unprecedented spontaneity had earned him any leniency. Her disapproval and resistance had only increased until she'd swung the wrecking ball of her "I quit" right into him.

And she'd meant it. He'd been certain she had.

Just as he'd thought he was down to coercion, she'd

done that most ridiculous thing, offering him the money she had on her. After his initial perplexity, it had been like a light had burst inside him, illuminating the tunnel of dwindling options she'd squeezed him in. How to end this impasse on a high note. His solution, not to mention its effect on her when he'd declared it, had brightened his mood in a way he hadn't felt in...ever.

Suddenly, the grin stretching his lips since he'd left her in that parking lot froze.

He might have decided to change the dynamics of dealing with her, but if he'd learned anything about Liliana Accardi so far, it was that she cared nothing about his power or wealth or what she could gain from them. To her, he was nothing but the invader who'd stormed into and defiled what she considered her home.

His parting shot might have been the worst thing he could have said. That defiant creature could now be working herself into a lather, more determined than ever not to return to the lab.

When the limo stopped, his mood was blacker than it had ever been, even during his worst days in The Organization.

Seething in uncharacteristic exasperation, he heaved out of the car and strode inside his mansion, thunderclouds roiling through his veins.

Damn that Liliana Accardi.

He'd picked her as the easy-to-tame lab rat, and she'd turned out to be an impossible-to-curb hellcat.

He had no time for a struggle with her. She wasn't even his target, just a means to an end. But instead of a solution, she'd turned out to be an insoluble problem.

If she insisted on defying him, he'd let her quit. But he'd make sure she'd find no other job in the country. Hell, on earth. She'd either work for him or she could go flip burgers. He'd put her in her place, doing exactly what he thought her good for. Then he'd search for a more ame-nable member of the Accardis as his bridge into that ac-cursed family.

It was only an hour later, under the beating needles of a punishing jet shower, when he found himself stroking a painfully hard erection to an explosive climax to the memory of the mutinous passion in Liliana's eyes, that he realized his plan was inapplicable.

Logic said he should consider her a lost cause. But this volcanic lust she'd provoked in him—more inexplicable because it was for her being, not her body, which he hadn't even properly seen—made it impossible for him to walk away from her or let her walk away from him. It was the last thing he'd thought would happen, but he *wanted* that aggravating, uncontrollable rebel.

It no longer mattered to him why he'd wanted to tame and acquire her in the first place. All that mattered to him now was that he did. For his own pleasure.

He'd never done anything for his own pleasure.

High time he did. And Liliana Accardi, that intractable creature, the first one to ever defy and spurn him, was the perfect place to start.

Lili ended the phone call with Brian and pinched the bridge of her nose, hard.

She didn't need this. Not after the night she'd had.

After Antonio Balducci had left her feeling punch-drunk, she'd driven home, garnering way more honks from disgruntled drivers than she usually did. She'd never got-ten used to driving in LA. Never gotten used to living in that house. All she could think of was it was time to let it all go. Let her mother's memory and everything she'd built in this city go.

That was all she could think when she could focus on anything but Antonio Balducci. When every word he'd said to her, every look, every inflection of his voice and peal of his laughter hadn't been revolving in her mind like a mini tornado.

She'd arrived at the house exhausted in a way she hadn't been since her mother's final days. But her fatigue hadn't been soaked with despondence, but with jittery restlessness.

Antonio had messed her up but good. And he'd known it. He'd almost skipped away knowing he'd shut her up and had the last word this time.

If she'd surprised him with her resistance, he'd shocked her with his response.

See you tomorrow, partner.

Indeed!

When she'd finally fallen asleep, she'd fallen into a turbulent realm filled with heart-hammering glimpses and whispers and touches. All of him.

She'd woken up burning and wet, sure he'd meant to invade her dreams. She'd never squirmed for release like that, but had drawn the line at seeking it. He could rule her subconscious, but she was damned if she'd consciously give him that power over her, even if only she would know about it.

At least that was what she'd told herself until she'd sought the relief of a hot bath and ended up bringing herself to an unprecedented orgasm to his memory.

Damn him.

She'd been still trembling with aftershocks when Brian had called her. Antonio had asked him to let her know their first management meeting was at two sharp.

At Brian's rabid curiosity, she'd said Antonio was just messing with her, as punishment for daring not to prostrate herself at his feet, like they'd all done. She doubted Brian bought that. Even when she believed it to be the truth.

She'd underestimated Antonio's need for control. He'd

pursued her to lasso her back when she'd dared be the only
one who didn't roll over and expose her belly. She'd struggled against his inexorable influence, trying to make him
consider her a troublemaker not worth the effort it would
take to subjugate her, to maintain his no doubt pristine
dominance record. That had only backfired, judging by
his parting shot.

Even then, she'd really thought she didn't have to worry
about him anymore. He might be obsessive when it came
to getting his way, but she was certain he was too busy
to bother with his employees again, especially rebellious
ones. She'd thought he'd walk away and forget all about
her, or remember her only as a weird creature who'd af-
forded him passing amusement. She'd been secure—and
oppressively let down—that she'd never see him again.

Then Brian had called.

Antonio hadn't been joking. Or maybe he had been,
and he hadn't finished yanking her chain yet. It appeared
she entertained him, and it was equally obvious he hadn't
had enough of her diversion yet.

Problem was, she had to oblige him.

He was the one to give her the end-of-service releases,
recommendations and payments. As much as she would
have loved to not look back, she needed all that to be able
to leave and survive until she found a new job.

After dressing in her most funereal outfit, she pulled
her unruly hair—which seemed to have more red in its au-
burn depths to go with her mood—in a severe bun. Forgo-
ing even the little makeup she usually wore, she winced
at her reflection.

Now that she was aware how she looked to others,
she could see that everything she felt was emblazoned
on her face. Aversion, aggression, anticipation and, dammit, arousal.

She shouldn't have given in to the urge to seek release. It

had done nothing but inflame her more. Her body throbbed like an exposed nerve, every movement triggering an avalanche of responses. Now sexual awareness was stamped all over her.

Hoping the drive to the lab would dampen her condition, she cursed herself, Antonio and the whole world and headed there. It felt like she was about to sever a chunk of herself and leave it behind. But she had to do it.

She'd try to continue her work elsewhere. If she couldn't, whatever she decided to do then would be her choice, not his. That it would be a choice he'd forced her into would still be better than being forced to do what he wanted now.

Arriving at the lab, she realized from everyone's unusually zippy behavior that he was there. Probably setting up his boss area for whenever he came to inspect. No doubt he was also expecting her to obey his directive. The rat had gotten to her through her best friend so he'd corner her.

Well, it hadn't worked. It was 4:00 p.m. already, and when he got the confrontation he wished for after she'd gathered her stuff, she'd make sure it would be their last face-off.

As she headed to her lab, she noticed everyone was looking at her differently, with incredulousness and something else…a new kind of courtesy, perhaps? The only explanation was that he'd taken his joke too far, had told everyone what he'd told her yesterday.

Annoyance with all of them, especially with him, mushroomed as she pushed into her lab…and felt as if her brain had hit a brick wall.

Antonio sat at her desk. His gaze collided with hers at once, as if he'd been waiting for her to walk in.

"Is this how late you'll be coming in from now on?"

Every nerve in her body fired at the combo of his jaw-dropping beauty and his teasing remonstration.

Before she could consider a comeback, he uncoiled to his formidable height, approached in that indolent predator's prowl, his lips twisting. "I didn't expect you to change to partner mode that quickly. But then you never do anything I expect. I like it. Immensely."

Forcing herself to move as he came to a stop before her, she unhooked her backpack and circumvented him. Without looking back at him, she started emptying her station, every nerve jangling in alarm as he came closer.

"Are you doing what I think you're doing?" When she didn't answer him, he harrumphed. "I enjoy your unexpectedness up to a point. That point is when you use it to deprive me of it. This, Dr. Accardi, I won't sanction."

Packing her last article, she yanked the zipper closed, then looked up. Though she'd braced herself, she felt gut-punched to behold his gorgeousness up close, now smoldering hotter with disapproving authority. Forcing steadiness into her stance, she pulled an envelope from her backpack's outer pocket, and thrust it out at him.

It was déjà vu when he glowered at it, but when he raised his eyes, there was no questioning. He knew what that was.

"I'm not accepting your resignation, Dr. Accardi." His lips crooked into that smile that had her insides liquefying. "Not to mention it would take far more than a piece of paper now to terminate our partnership."

Grinding her teeth at the throbbing between her legs, she thrust her other hand palm-up at him. This time, he raised a questioning eyebrow, making her want to yank that regal head down and bite that perfect wing of provocation.

"My three hundred dollars, please."

"Buying back your shares?" At her nod, he laughed, and her legs almost gave out. "You think your money spent a whole night with me and remained the same?"

Images bombarded her, of spending a whole night with

him and being changed forever. Even if he hadn't meant for her to think that, she did. The man was sex personified. She had to face the fact that she'd walk out of here, never to see him again, and would forever pleasure herself to his memory.

Gritting her teeth, she kept her hand outstretched. "My money, please. This is no longer remotely funny."

"It's the most fun I've ever had. And I don't have your money on me. I don't walk around with three hundred thousand dollars in my pockets."

Her mouth dropped open. "Not even you can multiply stock by a factor of a thousand overnight!"

"You'd be very impressed by what I can do over the course of one night." Her blood boiled over before he added, "But you're right. I was exaggerating. Your money is now around thirty thousand dollars. Still don't have that much on me."

"Keep it, capital and investment. Consider it my contribution to whatever good science you develop."

She had to get away from him. If she succumbed to him in any way, the damages he'd cause her would be worse than his wiping out three years of her work. This man could end her peace of mind. Could turn her into one of those women who groveled at his feet. It was getting harder with every breath to resist his spell and it wouldn't take him long to cast it fully over her. And while others seemed thrilled to be enthralled, it would destroy her.

But when she tried to walk around him, he blocked her, mischief frolicking in his eyes.

Stopping, she clutched her backpack harder. "Listen, Dr. Balducci. Enough, okay? I don't want to work for you, and I sure as hell am not your partner. Accept my resignation and give me what I ask for in this letter. I only ask for my rights."

"I don't care what you think your rights are." He silenced her protest by stepping closer, until the heat of his body and breath singed her. "I don't need to read this letter to know that you make a habit of shortchanging yourself. I, on the other hand, offer you what you really deserve."

That had her heart stuttering. "I only deserve to be left alone to continue my work. I never asked for anything more."

"And if I consider granting you this?"

And *that* had her heart skipping like a pebble over water. "Y-you would?"

"I would. On the condition that you become my partner."

She coughed a mirthless laugh. "I'm not even partner material for an ice-cream stand. I know nothing about running a business. If you're doing this to stop me from leaving for some reason only you'll ever know, I assure you, you don't need to bribe me with any bogus executive position I have no wish for and would be useless at. I'm probably the only person you'll ever meet who considers such a promotion a terrible fate and not a reward. But I'll gladly stay if you let me continue my work."

"So you're fine with me as your boss? You'd stay in spite of all your vigorous objections to me and my methods?"

"As long as you leave me alone, professionally and personally, I don't care if you're developing immunizations to sunlight for vampires and to silver for werewolves."

His lips split in such an exuberant smile, dazzling her with a flash of white teeth and searing charisma.

She was trying not to hyperventilate when he made it impossible, reaching out and slipping the backpack off her shoulder, his long, strong, capable fingers sliding against her flesh, making her core clench with violent need.

"Until we come to a new agreement," he said, "put your personal effects back where they belong."

She clung to the backpack as if to a life raft. "What new agreement? We didn't have an old one."

"Then we'll make a brand-new one from scratch."

With the utmost gentleness, he insisted on tugging the backpack out of her white-knuckled grip.

Letting it go felt as if she were lowering her last shield against him.

After placing it on her workstation, he faced her with a grin that had her swaying like a building in an earthquake. He leaned his hip on the desk, folded his arms over his expansive chest.

"Now that that's taken care of, there's something else I require."

"What's that?" she croaked.

"You. For dinner."

Four

"You want to have me for dinner?"

Lili hated that she'd squeaked. This man kept yanking at her composure. It was a matter of time before he snapped it.

"I meant I want to take you to dinner."

Her insides tightened more at his forbearing tone. "My IQ might be selective, but even I got that. Don't be—"

"—redundant? Yes, I know how you hate that." His gaze took on a new level of intensity. "But the other meaning is also right. Though I'd rather have you for dessert."

More convinced he'd decided to go all out having fun at her expense, she hissed, "Spare me the clichés, Dr. Balducci. And stop looking at me like that."

"Like what? Like you're the most fascinating thing I've ever seen? How can I, when you are?"

"That's what you tell yourself about the people you toy with? That they had it coming, being who they are?" She shook her head as his smile faltered. "But that's not how you're looking at me. At least, it's not how you're making me feel."

Every trace of levity left his face, avidness replacing it. "How am I making you feel? Tell me."

"You make me feel as if you're probing my every last thought."

His lips quirked, the smile back in his gaze. "Why would I do that when you wallop me over the head with everything that comes to your mind the moment it does?"

"It's what I've been asking myself, too, wondering why you bother. But you probably do it automatically. I think you go around scanning people to their molecular level and archiving your findings for future exploitation."

His eyes sobered. "So you don't think I do it for future reference, but for exploitation."

"Actually, I don't think it's only exploitation you're after, but flat-out mind control. You're not probing my thoughts, but trying to herd them where you want them to go. I can feel your mental tentacles trying to steer my brain."

His laugh was louder and longer this time. "Your unflattering opinion of me is devolving into sinister depths."

"I'm sure you don't care about anyone's opinion of you."

"I care about yours." The way he'd said that, his baritone caressing her inside and out... "Stop thinking it's your obligation to fight me on everything." His voice dipped another octave, making her very marrow vibrate. "Accept my dinner invitation, Dr. Accardi. I promise I won't eat you. No matter how tempted I am to do so."

Truth was, it was she who was tempted. To succumb to his persuasion. All she wanted was to say yes, to everything he was asking of her. Come what may.

She kneaded a throbbing temple, as if to stem her fast-dwindling common sense and willpower. "I don't know what's going on inside that convoluted mind of yours, Dr.

Balducci, and I really don't want to know. But whatever
it is, I know one thing. What you're doing here? It's a terrible idea."

His eyebrows shot up in imperious query. "It is? Why?"

Though she was certain he knew, she'd spell it out. She'd
give him whatever would make him leave her be, spare
her the tumult of his inexplicable interest.

"First, you're you and I'm me. Second, you're my boss,
until you accept my resignation. I'm against mixing professional and personal stuff. It always has catastrophic consequences, even when the professional situation is ideal,
not as problematic and hostile as ours."

"I have zero problems with you professionally. And the
last thing I am is hostile. I'm the very opposite."

"So I'm the hostile party. My bad."

His smile widened. "I like your hostility. A lot."

"Yeah, you find it hilarious."

"Tut-tut. I object to your insinuations that I'm having
fun at your expense."

"I'm insinuating nothing. You *are* having a ball."

"That I definitely am. You tickle my humor like no one
else. I say that without malice or condescension—just the
opposite. Like you, I say only what I mean."

"Really? I doubt that—about as much as I doubt my
ability to grow fur in winter." That earned her another
heart-palpitating chuckle that she did her best to ignore.
"If you said only what you mean, I don't think many in
your path would remain alive."

"So you're saying I'm tactful, even merciful?"

"Tactful? Maybe, but for your own ends only. Merciful? Sure. And I'm a flying manta ray."

A guffaw exploded from him, seeming to take him by
as much surprise as it did her.

His hand pressed his chest as if laughing hurt him.
Which it might, since he must be exercising muscles long

petrified from lack of use. She had a feeling not much amused him.

His other hand wiped at his eyes. "How does your mind come up with these things? Wait, don't answer. Mad scientist brain at work. And I thought I was one myself before meeting you. Turns out I'm too unimaginative to be one." When she groaned at his self-deprecation, his hands rose in a placating gesture. Then he leveled his hypnotic gaze on her, his lips still twitching, as if unable to stop smiling. "So if it's dubious I'm tactful, and certain I'm not merciful, what do you think I am?"

"You're inexorably diplomatic and inhumanly charismatic. And you wield both traits like weapons of mass manipulation. Not that I fault you for that. That *is* the best way of dealing with underlings for the best outcome. Why cultivate resentments and enemies among lesser beings when you can as easily foster worship and recruit willing slaves?"

"My diplomacy and charisma aren't getting me any worship or acquiring me any slaves in this room. They seem to work in reverse on you."

"Yeah, contrary to my norm, my reactions to you seem the total opposite of everyone else."

"So it's only me who has that effect on you." His eyes flared with something scalding...and smug?

Really? He craved ego-inflating strokes from her? He didn't get enough from everyone else?

Well, she wasn't contributing to the severity of his self-aggrandizing syndrome. And she wasn't letting him keep on trying to break through her barriers.

"*So* since it's clear you won't give me what I came here for, I'll leave you to your manipulation games with your new horde of worshipping followers. But do take this still. Consider it a souvenir."

Pushing the envelope in his hand, she skirted him to

retrieve her backpack. She rushed to the door, forcing herself not to take a last look at him, praying she'd make it out without stumbling. She was almost out when his rich voice had goose bumps storming all over her.

"What did you mean before when you said, 'You're you and I'm me'? What are we exactly?"

She waited until she was outside the door, safe enough to turn to him. Beholding his majesty for the last time, she suppressed a pang of regret and sighed.

"We're two different species."

Antonio watched Liliana Accardi disappear, battling the urge to hurtle after her, to drag her back, preferably thrown over his shoulder, swearing and scratching.

After he managed to get himself under control, he shook his head.

And he'd thought he'd already been beyond intrigued coming here. Now, after she'd defied him again, lambasted him as no one had ever dared to, then walked out on him like no one had done before, his condition had worsened exponentially.

He was hooked. For the first time in…ever.

All through this latest confrontation, he'd kept seeing himself capturing those lush lips, shoving her back onto that workstation she'd cleared, and having his way with her. All the way. Repeatedly.

He'd gotten hard the moment she'd walked in, and remained painfully so, even now. Even when he hadn't guessed what her body looked like under those drab clothes she wore like a camouflage. For the first time physical attributes didn't count to him. Coveting her essential self—something he'd never thought possible—took his arousal to a level he'd never experienced.

He stared down at the envelope she'd foisted on him.

To think he'd set this up thinking she'd be just a conduit. A means to an end.

But it had taken her only one confrontation to derail his meticulous plan. Not only was she the only to ever outright challenge him, but when he'd added the extra pressure of personal interest, the point when other women would have buckled breathlessly, she'd become even more resistant.

Amazing.

She hadn't even bothered considering his invitation. An invitation he'd never issued before, and that other women would kill for. She'd just scoffed it off and walked away. She would have done so without looking back if he hadn't asked her another question. She'd stopped only long enough to give him her final verdict.

We're two different species.

Shaking his head again, he headed back to her workstation, sat down in her chair. Though it was uncomfortable and creaky, it was the only place he wanted to be right now. It made him feel closer to her somehow. He'd take that comfort until he had the woman herself close once again.

If he even managed it.

That was another first. To be uncertain he could win someone over.

After a moment of grappling with this added complication, he tore open her resignation letter.

The wording was appropriate, yet it revealed her unbending spirit, that indomitable spark that fueled her unique persona. Yet with every letter, something tightened more behind his rib cage.

She was asking for far less than she deserved. Than the least contributor in this lab he'd acquired to be near her deserved.

He'd been right. This woman had no idea of her worth.

How had this happened? Why had she come to think this was her due? Who had made her feel worth so little?

Her life was an open book with very few lines, so there could be only two culprits. Her father was the foremost perpetrator. Knowing he'd let her grow up without caring to establish any relationship with her must have formed the early views of her self-worth. Her mother hadn't been the epitome of parenthood, either. She'd been a severely dysfunctional woman who had no right to limit her daughter to her very questionable care. After Liliana's early childhood, she'd become consumed in her work before falling prey to a debilitating mental disorder, repeating her husband's abandonment, albeit in different ways.

It explained a lot about Liliana. Those abandoned as children grappled with not only trust issues, but with sometimes crippling feelings of worthlessness all their lives. He knew that all too well, having been a discarded child himself.

But he'd been lucky. Unbelievably, The Organization had been a better place for a child to grow up than the biological family Liliana had been unlucky enough to be born to.

That meant his approach today had been another miscalculation. He'd thought if he showed her that his interest had become personal, it would soften her. When it had only made her more adamant, he'd thought she'd been alarmed at how fast he was moving, because of his reputation as an indiscriminating female magnet, which he'd cultivated to serve his purposes.

But it wasn't only this part of his public persona that repelled her. It was how she perceived all of him. And how she perceived herself in comparison.

Like no other woman he'd met, she was actually put off by his wealth and power. To her he was a taker, like her father, someone immersed in his own needs and greeds, who cared nothing about the devastation he left behind.

Then came the part concerning herself.

If she didn't value herself, as was evident from that letter, it stood to reason that she was unable to understand his interest in her. So she'd assigned him the most unsavory motive she could think of. That he was toying with her for his cruel entertainment.

What irony, that she suspected his manipulation when he'd already relinquished it.

He could just hear his brothers saying this turnabout only served him right, in punishment for his initial plan to use her. Not that they hadn't done the same in their day. At least Rafael and Numair. They had both initiated their relationships with the women who'd become their wives with self-serving motives.

Not that he wanted to end up with a wife. He just wanted to experience and satisfy those unprecedented urges this spitfire provoked in him. And he would pursue her to the ends of the earth till he did.

He probed those new motivations more deeply. Was he feeling this way only because she defied him and pulverized his plans and expectations?

The internal interrogation ended before it started.

No. That was what had lured him in initially. But he'd stayed and kept going deeper because of *her*. She was a conundrum. A genius in her field, she was also so insightful she'd sensed things about him that no one had before. And she kept none of her insights to herself. Yet with all her brilliance, she was socially awkward, had reclusive tendencies. But what had him at the mercy of this unknown and unstoppable compulsion was that inside that steel shell of resolve and resistance, he felt such vulnerable, untried softness.

It was *that* that made him want to eat her up.

But his need to break down the insulating walls she'd erected around herself, what she kept raising higher around him, was more than desire. More than his dominance de-

manding she bow to him like everyone did. It actually...
dismayed him, what she thought of him. Because it was
unnervingly accurate. She saw him more clearly than anyone, even Ivan.

He was suddenly no longer feeling self-satisfied being
who he was. Now he actually felt the urge to change, so
he could improve her opinion of him.

If anything had ever disturbed him, it was *that* thought.

Could he be getting soft and stupid like his brothers?
Behind the suave front he'd meticulously created, he'd always been the one with steel-enforced nerves and dia-
mond-coated insides. Not even this unpredictable fireball
could change that...could she?

Of course she couldn't.

And when he got her to succumb—and he definitely
would—not only would he remain unchanged, it would
still serve his original cause. There'd at least be that, once
his desire for her dissipated.

But then, he couldn't even imagine it doing so. From
the aroused condition he remained in just thinking of her,
it seemed his need for her wouldn't fade easily or soon.

Which suited him. He had all the time in the world.

He would savor her capture and her devouring, slowly,
thoroughly, as he'd never done anything in his life.

Lili woke up very late. It had been another restless night
filled with outlandish, feverish dreams starring Antonio
Balducci.

She'd woken up with a hammering heart and a cramping
core. She'd felt so needy that she'd barely refrained from
relieving the throbbing between her legs in the shower.

Getting out in record time before she succumbed to
temptation and ended up feeling only worse, she eyed the
pajamas she'd decided to spend the day in, shrugged list-
lessly and headed to the kitchen in her bathrobe instead.

She needed sugar. Lots of it. She'd bought giant triple chocolate chip muffins last night. Two for breakfast sounded
about right. It wouldn't compensate for the loss of her job
and security, but it would make her feel better nonethe-
less. Hopefully.

Flopping on the couch in front of the TV, she decided
she'd binge-watch every single episode of every sitcom she
liked. If that meant she'd sit there with only kitchen and
bathroom breaks for the next month, so be it.

By the fourth episode of her favorite show, she found
herself actually watching and not replaying her confrontations with Antonio in a never-ending loop. Soon she was
chuckling, then laughing, then reciting the lines that had
become engraved in pop culture. She was singing a jingle
alongside one of her favorite characters at the top of her
lungs when the bell rang.

Her raucousness came to a halt as her eyes darted to the
wall clock. At 1:00 p.m. on a Wednesday, the few neigh-
bors in her gated community who ever came knocking
knew she'd be at work.

It had to be one of them checking out the inexplicable
noises. Or the mailman leaving something she'd forgotten
she'd ordered online, as usual.

Coming to this conclusion, she turned the volume down,
subdued her hair and tightened the belt of the two-sizes-
too-big bathrobe. Failing to locate her slippers, she pat-
tered barefoot to the door.

She pulled it open, eyes down looking for a package.
Instead, they fell on a pair of big shoes. Polished, hand-
made ones.

Her eyes trailed up, over endless legs, a lean abdomen,
a door-wide chest and shoulders, all encased in darkness
that seemed to absorb the sunlight like a black hole.

"You're sitting at home watching sitcoms and causing

a neighborhood-wide alert, when you should be in your lab advancing medical science?"

Lili blinked, for a moment believing the colossus she was staring at was an apparition. Perhaps she'd been thinking of him so obsessively she'd actually conjured him.

Not that even her fevered imagination could replicate him. Antonio Balducci was really on her doorstep, glowing like a gilded god in the afternoon sun, perfect in ways that she hadn't known possible and that should be outlawed.

And there she stood in front of this vision of grandeur, the hair she hadn't combed a riot of tangles, no doubt looking like a freckled porcupine drowning in its parent's garment.

When she continued to gape at him, he folded his arms over his chest, his gaze mock-severe. "May I remind you that you didn't ask permission to take the day off?"

His reprimand finally snapped her out of her stupor. "May I remind you that I tendered my resignation?"

His majestic head jerked up in dismissal, presenting her with an even better view of his formidable jaw and cleft chin. "You may also remember it was categorically rejected."

She tossed her head back, too, attempting to emulate his haughtiness. "I needed you to approve my resignation only so you'd provide me with my end-of-service benefits. Your approval is unneeded if I relinquish them. Which I did. So I can do what I want. And I'm doing exactly that. Sleeping in and watching TV."

He gave such a pout, it was a wonder she didn't jump him to bite those maddening lips. "I hate to burst your bubble, but a rejected resignation only means you still work for me."

"No, it means I give up all the rights that come with an accepted resignation."

"Accepted resignations don't only come with benefits. They come with recommendation letters—"

She cut in. "I'll do without those, too."

He continued as if she hadn't interrupted him. "—endless severance forms to fill and to sign—"

She butted in again. "I'll do that sometime next week."

That made him stop, his gaze merrily roaming her, his lips twitching on the verge of ending his not-so-convincing stern act.

Yeah, tell her about how ridiculous she looked.

"Won't you invite me in?"

"No."

Her immediate answer gained her an equally swift "Why?"

"Because of all of the above."

His eyes twinkled in the sunlight, a more crystalline and intense blue than she'd ever seen. "It's not good for your health to hold a grudge."

"Oh, it's very cathartic to do so, for a limited time. I've allowed myself a week of hurling curses your way."

As his lips lost the fight and broke into a smile, the image burst in her mind of a lightning bolt striking him in that perfect ass. And she burst out laughing.

His eyes narrowed as he examined her. "Are you drunk, Dr. Accardi?"

"What if I am?" she spluttered. "I can't get a ticket riding my couch."

Without warning, he crossed her threshold.

A thousand alarms rang in her head. "Hey, you can't do that. I haven't invited you in."

He walked her back into her foyer, his advance slow, smooth, a sweep of power and seduction, the very opposite of her ungainly stumbling.

"Like a vampire, you mean?"

"I wouldn't be surprised if you were one."

"Then I would have certainly developed that anti-sun vaccine you mentioned before." He took another step closer. "I would have also developed a no-invitation-needed immunization."

Another few steps back had her thudding against something hard. The archway of the great room. Her heart bobbed in her throat as he bent his head closer and inhaled deeply, his eyes watching her intently.

"You smell of...you."

The way he said that, it was as if he were bracing himself against some sharp ache. His velvet groan was the darkest she'd heard his voice.

Trying not to let the shudder that traversed her body rattle it visibly, she smirked. "Thanks for the news flash. And here I always thought I smelled of someone else."

"Do you have any idea how you smell?"

"As long as I don't smell bad, who cares?"

"If you don't know who, I won't tell you. Yet." He lowered his head, closed his eyes and drew another deep inhalation. "I know now that defiance and dry wit and fearlessness have scents. Hot and sweet and bright." Before she decided if she'd swoon or not, he added, "You also smell of ginger and orange." He'd pinpointed the scents in her shampoo and conditioner. His eyes opened, heavy and hooded, filled with so much she couldn't understand but that still seared her to the marrow. "And chocolate."

Gulping, she nodded. "Yeah, I've overdosed on triple chocolate chip muffins."

"Sounds great. Smells better. Offer me some."

"What makes you think I have any left? Should I refresh your memory about the definition of *overdosed*?"

He gave her a perfect Bela Lugosi leer. "Should you be haggling with a hungry vampire who's doing you the courtesy of settling for chocolate instead of blood?"

"The hungry vampire will take the blood anyway, so I'm at least saving the chocolate."

Shaking his head in gesture of surrender, he laughed. Peal after peal of debilitating male amusement. That thick, corded neck jutting from his open black silk shirt was the closest it had been to her lips. It was so tempting, as if inviting her to reach up and sink her teeth—

Dammit. Get away!

Though he wasn't really crowding her, she sucked in her stomach as she squeezed out from between him and the wall. Grabbing the remote, she turned off the TV, then swung back to him. He'd followed her, was facing her across the couch.

"How about we dispense with the comic relief and get to the reason for your home invasion?"

"I came to resolve the issue that made you skip work today."

"For the last time, I skipped nothing. I quit."

"Yes, I got that the first time you said it. I'm here to tell you quitting isn't an option."

"It's my only option. You gave me ultimatums—"

"I offered you alternatives."

"—and I rejected them. So I was back to square one—working on your project and having mine swept aside."

He shook his head. "You keep making assumptions of what I think or what I'll do, and they're consistently inaccurate."

"What's inaccurate in all I said?"

"Only the most relevant part. Your assumption that I wasn't open to compromise. Which I certainly was. You pushed, I countered and our negotiations were just starting when you took off."

"There was nothing more to negotiate."

"There's always more. Nothing is ever final."

"I thought with you everything is."

His gaze swept her from head to toe and back, swathing her in fire. "I thought so, too. But I'm learning that was because I never found a worthy challenger."

"Me? Yeah, right."

"I will cure you of that self-deprecation yet. For now, I'm here to tell you that you can have your project back, with all the logistical support and financial backing I would have offered you to work on mine. I ask for nothing in return."

Her mouth fell open but nothing came out.

It was only on the third attempt that she croaked, "So what's the catch?"

"You're *assuming* again."

"Just spit it out. The one thing I can't handle is surprises. I have to know what I'm walking into while I'm still a thousand miles away."

His eyes gleamed with approval. "A control freak, I see."

"Takes one to know one. But then again, I'm just a wannabe who has nothing to show for my obsessive proclivities. You're the real deal with the billions to prove it."

"Again, you shortchange yourself." He frowned for a moment before he exhaled. "There's no catch, Dr. Accardi. Your pressure tactics worked."

"What pressure tactics?"

His huff was incredulous. "Seems it's not only me who does things on autopilot. You flat-out bulldozed me."

"I was only struggling not to let you bulldoze me."

"And your struggle was so ferocious you upended the tables. It took me a while to realize I was beaten, since it never happened before. But there's a first time for everything. So here I am, coming with a white flag. If there's one thing I ask, it's that you promise you'll separate our professional and personal interactions from now on."

"We have no personal interactions."

"Something I aim to rectify, starting now, over lunch."

"What is it with you and meals?"

"We do have to eat. We'll eat together."

It was her turn to shake her head, disbelief coursing through her. She'd expected him to consider her a pest, to dismiss her and spare her his disconcerting focus. But not only had he come after her again, but the more obnoxious she was, the more patient and persuasive he grew.

But for whatever reason he was doing this, there was only so much temptation she could withstand.

Clinging to the last vestiges of sanity, she exhaled. "You must be in dire need of amusement. But let's say I accept, how about something quick? Coffee? Here?"

He shook his head, unmovable. "Lunch. Out."

"I'll give you a muffin."

His laugh rang out again, and she could swear all of her mother's crystal still distributed around the living area where she'd left them sang in response.

He was still chuckling when he persisted, "Lunch. A leisurely one. So clear your agenda."

"What agenda? I'm unemployed now."

"You're no such thing. We're celebrating your triumphant return to your lab. This is nonnegotiable, Liliana."

Her heart somersaulted. It didn't matter that it was impossible. It did. Then it attempted to burst out of her chest.

At her distressed cough, he covered the distance between them urgently, held her by the arms, solicitous, singeing her even through the thick terry cloth.

"Are you all right?" When she nodded and tried to step away, he followed, hands tightening on her arms. "Liliana…"

"Lili." It was too much hearing him say her full name, making it an overpowering spell. "If you're no longer calling me Dr. Accardi, then call me Lili like everyone else."

An eyebrow rose imperiously. "You're Liliana to me and I will always call you that. That is also nonnegotiable."

Stepping back so she could breathe again, she raised her hands. "Okay, okay, call me whatever you want. I will call you whatever I want, too."

"And what's that?"

"I didn't mean to your face."

His guffaw was more delighted than ever. "And what will you call me outside of your internal rants?"

"I'd rather not call you at all."

He took her arm again, steered her toward the ground-floor bedroom where she slept. "Call me anything you want. I eagerly anticipate whatever you come up with. Now go dress."

"I haven't said I'll go out to lunch with you."

"You will."

"Is this the billionaire's entitlement or the surgeon's god complex, or were you just born an overbearing brat?"

He whooped in laughter again. "You'll get a chance to find out over lunch. Now go put on something nice."

She yanked her arm from his grip. "I don't have something nice. Not by your standards."

"Anything that doesn't smother you in layers of cloth."

"I don't have that, either."

"Anything not hideous. I'm sure you can manage that."

"This bathrobe isn't hideous. Would you settle for that?"

"I would. Would you?"

She should go out with him in her bathrobe and bare feet and see if he'd still take her to lunch.

Her thoughts paused before she huffed in resignation, threw her hands up and headed to her bedroom.

She'd bet he wouldn't bat an eyelid. If she even stripped naked it wouldn't deter him. Or maybe *that* would change his mind about taking her out and he'd—

Oh, shut up. He'd nothing. All this was probably him conducting some experiment, and he considered her the perfect test subject.

After that lunch, and after he was sure she'd go back to
work, she doubted she'd see him again. Even had he been
interested in her *that* way, Antonio Balducci had perfected
the art of the one-night—or the one-outing—stand.

So what would one lunch hurt, anyway? She should actually make the most of it.

It would be her first and last chance with him.

Five

She'd worn something nice.

As nice as she could manage from a wardrobe designed for a life that had no social or romantic components.

Not that she'd thought it was nice when she'd put on the dark green sleeveless above-knee dress with matching three-inch sandals.

That verdict was his.

When she'd come out of her bedroom, flushed because he'd been across from her door when she was totally naked, he was watching the same sitcom episode she had been when he'd arrived.

He'd thrown his head back like a lazy feline, then had said one word. *Nice.*

The word itself was innocuous enough. It had been the way he'd looked at her and the way he'd said it, that lethal gaze and that purr of bone-liquefying seduction, that had swept her in flames of longing.

Not that she thought that was his objective. Seducing

her was too far-fetched a motive behind everything he'd done so far. Her amusement factor remained the most probable reason.

She reeled all over again at the cascade of events that had led her to this point, where she was sitting beside him in his luxurious Lamborghini.

When he'd found her eyeing everything as if she feared touching it, he'd only said that he always bought Italian-made cars, as a nod to his heritage—which she shared. Knowing he was trying to disprove her "different species" comment without tackling it head-on, she'd countered that he found this car appealing not because of its country of origin but its million-dollar price tag. He'd only sighed about her continued gross misjudgments and, with a wiggle of an eyebrow, *under*estimates.

Feeling it would be obnoxious to criticize his personal spending habits, she'd instead questioned the absence of his limo and chauffeur. His response had been yet another blow to her equilibrium. That he hadn't been about to pick her up for their first lunch together with another man around.

Another woman would have been flattered out of her mind, with all sorts of ludicrous hopes soaring. *Her* response had been to stress what self-preservation dictated this should be—their first *and* last lunch together.

He'd given her an enigmatic look and let her statement stand. Either he agreed, or he'd let her say whatever she wanted because he knew he'd get his way in the end anyway.

Now she stole another glance at his sonnet-worthy profile as he negotiated a stretch of unruly traffic in downtown LA. Questions spun faster inside her mind.

What exactly was his way? What could he want with her? It couldn't be her as a woman that he was after. Could it?

Okay, so she was pretty enough, in what people called an unusual way. She'd had lots of interest from good-looking and successful guys. It had been her who'd been uninterested. A romance, or even a hookup, with all promised upsides, hadn't been worth the consequences she'd obsessively calculated.

But in comparison, *any* guy was a straggly tomcat to this majestic lion beside her. Whatever her attractions to men, she couldn't be up to *his* standards, not when he waded among the rare beauties of the world and didn't give even them the time of day.

That brought her back to her one plausible theory. That she entertained him like none had ever done, intrigued him because she hadn't fallen at his feet, and was still challenging him with every breath. Even as she melted inside.

"We're here."

His deep drawl jerked her out of her musings as he brought the car to a smooth stop. He sprang from the low-slung car fluidly, then rushed around to help her out. Her exit from the car was nowhere as seamless as his, his boost compromising her balance more, landing her against his unyielding strength.

He steadied her, that disturbing intimacy flaring in his eyes, and every primal urge in her fiercely wished she could remain engulfed in his heat and dominance and security.

As her ingrained aloofness kicked in and she stepped away from his support, a valet rushed to take the car away. Assorted other men in formal suits—she counted six—descended from two cars and stood at varying distances, clearly his bodyguards.

Following the trajectory of her gaze, Antonio sighed as he guided her over the curb to wide marble stairs. "That's my partner Richard being overprotective. He's Black Cas-

tle Enterprises' security specialist, and his men follow us
every second, till we die. If it's up to him, we never will."

Something dreadful lurched inside her at the thought
of such an indomitable being dying.

His gaze stilled on her face, as if he'd felt the intensity
of her reaction and was probing her mind for its cause. "I
hope it's not bothering you."

She blinked up at him as they ascended the stairs toward an ornately carved mahogany double door. "Why
should it?"

"Because you're out with a man who allegedly needs
that much protection. Not a comforting thought, I'm sure."

That was what he'd thought had dismayed her?

Not that she could fault his inaccuracy. She'd given him
no reason to think she'd be disturbed at the thought of his
death. But she was, jarringly so.

"When we try to make him lay off, Richard tells us
we're lucky he posts guards at that distance. It's pointless
arguing with him when his only alternative is 24/7 sur-
veillance much closer up."

"He has a good reason for his vigilance," she murmured.
"You're too high-profile. You're as recognizable as any
Hollywood celebrity, and much more influential. There
must be many people whose lives would be easier with
you out of the way."

She fought not to clutch his arm in reflex protection
as two doormen opened the doors for them. She hoped
he'd tell her that she watched too many action movies,
that paranoid prophylactic measures were merely part of
his partner's job.

As if diagnosing her anxiety right this time, his gaze
gentled. "As you so keenly observed before, I never make
enemies. I also make sure it's in everyone's best interest to
keep me around and healthy. I'm in no danger whatsoever."

"Really?"

pUSHAGE

His smile broke out again, brightening her mood at once after the sharp dip it had taken. "Really."

Believing him, she exhaled her pent-up breath. "But the valet is *your* man. You wouldn't trust someone you haven't picked and vetted yourself with that car of yours."

His eyes glowed, though with what she couldn't diagnose. Whatever it was, a girl could get addicted to it, could get lost in it, and be lost without it.

"*That's* the mind I wanted working on my projects."

"An hour ago you considered that that mind jumps to rash and unsubstantiated assumptions."

"Only when it comes to my motives. We did agree I invert your thought process. How about you try to keep it upright from now on?"

"I don't do it on purpose, you know. But I'll try for the duration of lunch. Should be easier when I'm busy eating."

He swept an arm forward to usher her inside. "Then by all means, let's eat."

The restaurant he'd chosen turned out to be a place she hadn't known existed in the city she'd lived in for the past eight years. Inside a building she'd passed a hundred times before.

On the outside, it looked like any other upscale building in LA. On the inside, it made any other grand place she'd ever been inside look shabby. It wasn't only the old-world, aristocratic luxury, but the very atmosphere radiated mystery and exclusivity. She kept expecting to see James Bond and his gallery of villains walking through the hyper-real setting.

But then, next to the god who led her deeper into his domain, every other larger-than-life character, real or fictional, would fade to nothing.

As they made their way deeper into what had to be a club of some sort, everyone in their path, each clearly hailing from a world of extreme breeding and wealth, exclaimed reverential greetings. Some actually bowed.

And she'd thought the Italian clan she belonged to by birth, who'd recently burst into her existence, was the epitome of elitism. But Antonio's affluence, not to mention the awe he commanded, far surpassed the Accardis.

Not that wealth or power were of any interest to her. Her family's or his. The only reason she was debating entering her father's world was so she would have the family she'd never had. As for Antonio, the trappings of fame and fortune actually detracted from the far more impressive man cloaked in them.

With a hand on the small of her back, he led her into a ballroom-sized room with only one table for two in the center, exquisitely set in silk, silver and crystal. Her mind boggled at what it took to empty such a place and reserve it exclusively, at such short notice. If he didn't keep it perpetually reserved for himself, that was.

He'd just sat down opposite her when her phone vibrated with a loud buzz in her purse. Still jangling from Antonio's gossamer touches as he'd seated her, she almost jumped.

His hand rose in pure graciousness, permitting her to take the call, but his eyes remained fixed on her, letting her know he'd give her no privacy.

Getting the phone out, she fumbled it in unsteady hands, mumbled her chagrin at him, and herself, under her breath. It came out louder than she'd intended, since it elicited a blinding flash of his teeth.

She reeled in her runaway reactions, groaning as she saw the caller ID. Not the best time to talk to the *other* man who caused her emotional upheavals.

The moment she croaked a hello, her father's voice burst into her ear. "*Mia bella* Lilianissima, how are you, *tesoro*?"

Lili winced. Her father's over-the-top enthusiasm never ceased to jar her. It was weird he'd be so vocally eager after a lifetime of not even acknowledging her existence. It was even more unsettling after her mother's detached treatment, and the fact that Lili had been raised to think her father and the whole Accardi clan had ice water running in their blue-blooded veins. Recently, everything had been one contradiction after the other.

She took a breath and steadied her voice before she spoke. "I'm fine, Alberto. How are you?"

"*Tesoro*, when will you start calling me Padre or Daddy?"

She licked her lips, Antonio's vigilance intensifying her nervousness. "Maybe one day I can manage Father…"

"Then make that day today, *tesoro. Per favore!*"

"Uh, listen, Albe… Father…" She paused as her father celebrated her capitulation on the other end with another deluge of endearments. "I'd love to talk, really, but I'm at lunch with…an associate." Antonio's eyes glowed with something that made the electricity surging through her system spike. "I'll call you when I get home. Or tomorrow. With our time difference it must be already very late for you."

"I'm not in Venice, *tesoro*. I'm in New York City. Among the reasons I'm calling you is to tell you all the US-based Accardis are anxious to meet you. They're holding a reception in your honor in our main ancestral home here."

She almost blurted out a refusal. Not that she expected such an event to be unpleasant. So far every Accardi her father had introduced to her had been gracious and welcoming. Either her mother had falsely advertised the family in order to explain why they never had anything to do with them, or they were accommodating her father's fervent desire to include her in their exclusive ranks. Up till now, though, she'd met the Accardis one or two at a time. The idea of meeting them en masse was enough to give her performance anxiety.

"Is this weekend good for you?"

"No." The response came out far sharper than she'd intended. Biting her tongue, she tried again. "I...have work to do."

"On the weekend?"

Her gaze again clashed with Antonio's watchful one, then saw the satisfaction there. Her blood heated to the point where she felt steam rising off her body.

"Our lab has been taken over, and our new taskmaster has turned things upside down. I'm behind in my schedule because of his antics, and I have no idea when I'll get caught up."

Antonio's grin became as wide as she'd ever seen it as he beckoned to a waiter bearing champagne chilling in an ice-filled antique silver bucket.

Narrowing her eyes, she moved to end the call. One turmoil-inducing man at a time was her limit.

"Please let them know I'm unavailable this weekend before they put any plans in motion. When I sort out my stuff here, we'll discuss this further, okay?"

"Certamente, tesoro. Call me whenever it's convenient for you. Don't worry about the time difference or any other considerations. Wake me up, interrupt my meetings, anything at all. Talking to you is far more important than anything else. I have a lifetime of unmade calls I need to make up for."

To that she grumbled something vague around the lump that suddenly filled her throat and ended the call.

As she put her phone away, struggling to swallow through the tightness, Antonio poured champagne in her crystal flute and handed it to her.

"Your father?"

She grimaced. "Rhetorical questions fall under my redundancy ban. My father was so loud you must have heard his every word. And you heard me call him Father."

He also no doubt knew everything about her personal life, such as it was. Who her father was and that she'd grown up without him must have been the first things in the dossier he must have on her as he had on everyone in his employ. He probably knew the recent developments, too. He just wanted her to elaborate with her own version of details and updates.

At his unrepentant, probing stare, she sighed. "Yeah. My father. Long-absent and recently very much present. Therefore the extreme enthusiasm. He'll cool off, eventually. But for now I'm the daughter he reconnected with, all grown-up minus the hassle of years of teething, tantrums and teenage angst."

That still, strange expression on his face deepened before he exhaled. "This is another thing that proves we're not two different species at all."

"What? That I happen to have an Italian father, too?"

"And that you grew up without said father."

"You…" Suddenly the lump was back in her throat. It was ridiculous, when she'd never really considered herself unfortunate, but imagining the boy Antonio had been growing up fatherless…hurt.

It was clear *he* wasn't going to elaborate. Which was fine by her. Though curiosity burned inside her, she didn't want to learn anything that would make her stupidly ache more on his behalf.

To assuage the pain she suffered now, she gulped a big mouthful of silky champagne. "That sort of barely puts us in the same genus."

He toasted her with his flute. "At least it's a step up the ladder toward us occupying the same evolutionary status." Taking a sip, he put his glass down. "But we do share far more than that. We're both doctors—"

"Who've trodden diametrically different paths, have opposing approaches, and reached incomparable results."

Undeterred, he continued as if she hadn't interrupted him in this volleying rhythm between them they seem to have perfected. "We're both unyielding—"

"Yeah, that's why I'm sitting here having lunch with you in this top secret hideout for billionaires and spies and not watching my sitcoms as I wanted."

"And that's why you made me bow to your demands without any of my own objectives realized in return."

Her lips twisted. "So you say."

"So it *is*. This round is all yours." He beckoned to the maître d' without taking his gaze off her, a new heat entering his eyes. "But don't think you're going to win every time."

His warning made it sound as if their interactions would continue beyond this lunch, or her going back to work.

A thrill of disbelief, dread and expectation buzzed through her all during their ordering process.

As soon as the maître d' left, Antonio sat forward, his eyes growing somber, worsening her condition. "There's just one thing I'm confused about."

She took another sip to relieve her drying mouth. "You get confused like mortals?"

His smile didn't reach his eyes this time. "No, I don't, actually. But you affect me in unprecedented ways. You confuse the hell out of me. Therefore my inability to understand how you would seek the father who abandoned you. I have firsthand knowledge of how you can do without anything or anyone. Not to mention how unforgiving you are."

"You describe me like *such* a well-rounded sociopath."

"I describe myself, too. More things we have in common."

"Things of which I have a drop while you have an ocean." She fell silent until the waiters placed soup in front of them and left. "But you're right, as usual. I had no intention of seeking him out. I lived my life without him and his family, and I never wished to change that. It took him months of persistence after my mother's death until I finally agreed to see him."

That earlier strangeness returned, deeper now, as if that piece of information disturbed him. Which made no sense.

Suddenly famished, for food or other things, she sought the refuge of the soup and changed the subject.

For the rest of what turned out to be the most incredible meal she'd ever had, they talked about so many other things, never again broaching anything personal.

After lunch he insisted on taking her to another place for coffee. Another place where he was treated like a god, and where she almost felt it was sacrilegious for her to be. And again, the place had only them.

She finally had to comment. "You emptied the restaurant at your exclusive club, and this place, too, for only us, didn't you?" He only nodded. "Why? Do you have something against eating in other people's presence?"

"I ate in yours quite successfully, as I recall." He leaned back in his seat, regarding her with that intentness she'd come to expect but would never get used to. "I wanted you to relax without intrusions or distractions."

"I *am* known for being around human beings without any adverse reactions." She shook her head, picked up her cappuccino cup, the finest china she'd ever touched. "But you're way stronger than I am. Apart from the evident ways."

"Care to explain that statement?"

"You can stomach all this over-the-top luxury and sycophancy. I wouldn't be able to, even on an occasional basis. It's actually one of the reasons I'm so reluctant to get any deeper into my father's life. Like you, he lives in a rarefied world where I can't belong."

* * *

Antonio stared at Liliana and again felt everything spinning even further out of his control.

He'd orchestrated that lunch to give her a taste of what it would be like to be with a man of his caliber. Though his money and power had no effect on her when her research hung in the balance, he'd thought when she was made their beneficiary on a personal level, it would be different.

But the more he immersed her in its benefits, the more repulsed she was by the evidence of his status. She'd made sideway remarks through the past hours, but now she'd come right out and said it. Being in such surroundings, getting the treatment only limitless wealth bought, disturbed, not dazzled, her.

Taking another sip of cappuccino, she shrugged. "To each his own, of course, but I don't see why you need to exercise your power in such ways."

He gritted his teeth on another unknown sensation. Chagrin. "Maybe I was trying to impress you."

A not-too-delicate snort made her put down her cup before she spilled its contents. "You thought this would impress me? Have you met me?" She sat forward, her eyes wide and earnest. "You know what *really* impresses me? It's that if you were stripped of all your financial assets right this second, with that brain of yours, filled with all your knowledge and experience, with those hands that perform miracles on a regular basis, your worth wouldn't be affected. Anything you lost, you'd re-create, bigger and better, because luck and circumstances played no role when you first created it. So no, this—" she swept a hand around "—doesn't impress me. If anything, all this glitter and bustle doesn't become you, actually taints your true value. Without any of those trappings, it's you on your own, your gifts and abilities, that's invaluable."

Something swelled inside his chest until he couldn't

breathe. So he didn't, let himself succumb to those whiskey eyes as they penetrated him to his core with their absolute truthfulness.

No one besides his brothers had ever treated him without artifice. But their candor had been nothing like this. It was indescribable being exposed to hers. Her ruthless bluntness at once slapped him for being a pathetic show-off and bestowed on him the most validating evaluation of his life.

He got adulation wherever he went, but no one had ever told him anything like that. That his intrinsic value remained unchanged without everything he'd achieved or acquired. It was what he'd told himself since he'd escaped The Organization. That his abilities would bring him success, would amass fortune and power, would re-create them if he ever lost them. But only Liliana had ever expressed that exact same belief in him.

And she did so when she still considered him an antagonist. She was fair enough that she'd give even an enemy his full due.

She raised her cup to her lips. "Though I commented because you dragged me to this creepily empty seven-star establishment, I hope you don't always feel the need to flaunt your wealth and impose your worth on the world. I assure you you're the last man on earth who needs to do that."

He finally exhaled his pent-up breath. "I'll be sure to make a note of that."

So not only had he failed to impress her, she'd ended up counseling him.

To make things worse, he'd totally lost track of time. Six hours had passed, when he'd intended to tantalize her for only a couple of hours and leave her wanting more, so next time she'd be more eager, or at least, less resistant.

But he'd been incapable of ending the most enchanting day he'd ever had, the most exhilarating duel he'd ever waged. He'd been swept on the tide of their affinity, the hunger that had been building inside him demanding more of her. It now craved all of her. Now, not later.

She pushed her cappuccino cup away. "Was that leisurely enough for you?"

"Not quite."

"C'mon, you said lunch, and it's now time for dinner."

"Then we have dinner. At a place of your choosing."

"You think it's possible for me to eat anything else? I can barely breathe. But you're a big boy who needs his nutrition, so you go ahead. I'll walk back home." She tapped her slightly curved belly through that dress whose color made her skin glow and her hair and eyes sparkle with red and gold fires. "I can sure use a long, hard walk."

"So we'll walk together. Then I'll drive you home." She started to object and he cut her off. "You don't think I'd let you go back home on your own, do you?"

"Why not? I've been doing it since I was a kid."

"You're not doing it on my watch." Before she could say anything else, he was on his feet, his hand extended to her.

Though she grumbled that he was an entitled chauvinist, she gave him her hand. It was all he could do not to yank her by it, slam her against his aching body and drink her dissension dry.

As they stepped out into the night, the warm, humid ocean breeze was so strong it swept her curls across his face. He groaned, getting another whiff of her scent, which had almost had him pouncing on her back in her house. His hardness had long crossed from painful to agonizing.

Giving in, he reached out to catch those locks. He'd send his plans of taking it slow to hell, would capture her by that lush cascade of silk, push her against the nearest building and devour her.

But she aborted his feverish intentions, pulling her locks away, one from between his lips. And their hands touched.

Jerking hers away as if he'd electrocuted her, she mumbled that her hair came alive in the wind, produced a clip from her purse and secured her rioting hair in an improvised updo.

Triumphantly declaring the problem contained, she starting walking. It took him a moment to get his stiff legs to fall into step with her. His breath had clogged in his chest so hard again he had to force himself to breathe.

That tightness increased all through their two-hour walk down the bustling streets. As did his enjoyment.

They argued, agreed, bickered and shared companionable silences. He even got her to laugh many times, once so hard she shed tears.

Getting her to lower her guard enough with him, then to respond to his wit and teasing so unreservedly, was the most rewarding thing he'd ever done.

Then to his dismay, she said that her feet were starting to hurt, being so unused to heels. He should have considered this, at least realized her discomfort when she'd slowed down. Not only had he been inconsiderate but now their walk had to end.

He offered to carry her so they could go on, and she laughed it off, thinking he was joking, which he wasn't. He called Paolo to deliver his car, and she took her sandals off while they waited, so he did scoop her up. No matter how much she spluttered for him to put her down, he insisted he wasn't letting her stand barefoot in the street.

Once driving, every cell of his body on fire, he kept wondering how he'd prolong the drive and his time with her.

He didn't want this night to end.

Then he felt her looking at him. At the next light he turned to her, found her gaze fixed on him with what looked like distressed embarrassment.

The tightness he was getting used to feeling around her returned in full force. "What's wrong?"

Her lips twisted. "Just that you went to great lengths to show me a good time and I was only a rude jackass in return."

"You only said what you thought without filters."

"Which is the definition of rudeness. I played back our whole outing and I realized you've been nothing but gracious while I've been obnoxious. At first I was so on purpose, but then I decided to stop, and I was still downright offensive."

"You were no such thing. You even paid me the biggest compliment anyone ever has. To everyone I *am* my success and power and money. You're the only one who ever thought I am the one who gives worth to my achievements and assets." Those wide eyes he never wanted to stop staring into grew larger. He gritted his teeth as he had to turn back to the road and drive again. "And even if you've been rude, I would have deserved it, since you consider I've coerced you into this outing."

"You didn't. I know I could have said no. But I did want to come. And I did enjoy everything, because I was with you. You're the best company I've ever had."

His gaze swung to her, caught her expression as she'd said these unbelievable statements.

Had he ever thought her anything less than the most perfect thing he'd ever seen? Was that how she truly felt? Could he be that lucky?

And whatever remained of his premeditation snapped. "I don't want to drive you home, Liliana. Come with me to mine."

The moment the words were out, he wanted to kick himself.

This was the last thing he should have said. He'd barely gotten her to trust him enough to enjoy being with him and to admit it. And he had to go and crash through her limits like an overeager teenager.

Now she wouldn't only refuse, she'd swat him back to persona non grata status. Women usually played demure at this point, so men wouldn't think them easy. But *her* refusal would be the most legitimate response ever.

Amidst the fury of self-disgust, he almost missed her answer. Braking too abruptly at the light, jerking her in her seat, he turned to her, disbelieving.

"What did you say?" he rasped.

Looking up at him without the slightest trace of guile, she repeated what he hadn't believed he'd heard her say.

"I said okay."

Entering Antonio's sprawling mansion a fraught half hour after he'd asked her to go home with him, Lili still wondered if she was having another wish-fulfillment dream. One far more detailed and realistic…and outrageously ambitious. She kept wondering if she'd wake up any moment now.

But the dream continued, tangible, all-encompassing, like his heat at her back, his aura intoxicating her like the champagne had failed to. Everything was way over the top.

Problem was, it was really happening. He'd asked her to come home with him and she'd accepted. In embarrassing speed and eagerness.

"Would you like a drink?"

She swung around at his quiet question, almost losing her balance, and found him watching her with the most unreadable glance he'd leveled on her so far. Every fiber in her body quivered. He'd been almost silent since she'd said okay. Now the way he regarded her… What was he thinking?

To give herself space, to figure out what to feel or do, she nodded. With an even more disturbing glance, he nodded back as his powerful hand loosened his tie and undid a button as if they were suddenly suffocating him. Her dry throat convulsed as she watched him turn away, cross the lavish, ultramasculine great room to a wet bar at its end, his every movement sheer poetry of grace and control.

Her mind raced as he prepared their drinks, every now and then saying something that only necessitated mono-syllabic responses from her.

She was now convinced he was interested in her. As a woman. Also known as sexually. While she could tell him he couldn't have picked a worse candidate for such interest, she doubted he'd listen. His intense fixation on her had only grown at her attempts to dissuade him from coming closer.

Maybe because he could talk to her, or she jogged his jaded senses, or she was a type he'd never encountered. Whatever the reason, he was interested.

But *interest* was too mild a word, insultingly so, to de-scribe what he provoked in her.

She *craved* him.

When she'd never wanted anyone. Or anything, for that matter. Besides scientific discovery. Not that she'd ever felt anything this out of control for science.

Still, mere craving didn't describe her feelings now. Every last component of her being was aroused. Her mind, her senses, her body. She was in an uproar. For him. Only ever him.

But while his interest had grown directly proportion-ate to her resistance, since she'd stopped resisting him back there in his car, something had changed. He'd been almost…subdued.

Had he regretted inviting her here the moment she'd agreed? Had he only done so because, based on her be-havior so far, he'd fully expected her to decline? Was he already losing interest now that she'd suddenly stopped providing him with the only things that had attracted him to her, resistance and surprises?

This probably explained the way he was behaving now.

Even if it didn't, she knew if she capitulated and joined his worshipping hordes, he *would* lose interest in her and move on. Sooner would be better than later. The longer she was exposed to him, the more severe the havoc he'd leave in his wake.

That led her to one possible decision. She'd give him what he expected as his right from all mortal beings.

He was sauntering back now with the drinks, as if he were postponing reaching her as much as he could. Stopping two steps away, when he'd always kept only one between them, he brooded down at her as he handed her a glass.

Gulping down agitation and regret, she took it. Then she reached for his glass, too. His eyes widened as he unclasped the glass and let her take it. Trembling in earnest now, she put the glasses down on a nearby coffee table.

His expression was perplexed when she straightened. It became stunned when she covered the space he'd kept between them, then reached up and pulled the tie he'd fully undone right off.

Dropping it to the ground, she lowered her eyes, unable to take the brunt of his blazing eyes this close up, or his disappointment that she'd turned out to be like every other woman he'd ever met. Squeezing her eyes shut, she did what she'd been aching to do since she'd laid eyes on him.

Sliding her hand beneath his shirt, she longingly glided her shaking, prickling hand over his hot, hard flesh.

Six

Antonio felt his mind short-circuiting.

Liliana. She was touching him. Igniting him into an uproar. Shocking him into paralysis.

This wasn't even among the things he'd expected or hoped for. He'd planned to court her, to break down her resistance in stages. But with a single "okay," she'd thrown everything out of whack. He felt like he'd been pushing with all his strength against an immovable object when suddenly all resistance was removed. He found himself hurtling with unstoppable momentum, falling flat on his face.

He'd still been struggling to adjust his thinking, and his actions accordingly as he'd handed her that drink, when she'd thrown him for a loop again by taking his, too, then proceeding to whisk off his tie. As the silk had hissed against his neck, as if relieved to part with his shirt, he'd frozen, his every sense converged on her eyes, trying to fathom from her expression what the hell had been going on.

But they'd been turbid with so many emotions. He *thought* he'd seen shyness, uncertainty, resignation, reck-lessness…and hunger, before she'd closed them as if to escape his analysis. Not that he could have been certain of anything. His mind had been a tangled mess by then.

And that was before she'd *touched* him.

Now a small, delicate hand slid beneath his shirt, as if searching for his heart. He felt as if she'd found it, taken hold of it. It was the only explanation for why it boomed in erratic thunder, when it had always remained steady in emergencies and under literal fire.

Her touch was like nothing he'd ever felt. It was like *he'd* never been touched before, and her tentative softness was his first exposure to human contact, to sensual stimu-lation. Sensations he'd never felt before exploded within him, detonating every single barrier inside him. The last dam was his control.

He was no longer in command of his thoughts or reac-tions, nor did he want to be. Of its own accord, his hand clamped her wrist, stopping the torment of her touch. Her eyes jerked open and up, alarm and mortification spread-ing in their gold depths. And his last thread of restraint snapped.

A primal rumble surging from his depths, he did what he'd wanted to do every second of the past three days. He yanked her against his body, hard. He growled something incoherent at the music of her cry, enveloping her in his arms and crushing her against him.

For one suspended moment, their gazes merged. Hers was at once stunned and surrendering. His heart felt as if it would explode if he didn't possess those lips that spilled those mind-melting sounds of submission.

"Antonio…"

He swooped down, his open mouth swallowing her gasp as he drove his tongue between her lips and plumbed her depths. The taste and scent of her, both overpowering aphrodisiacs, made him growl again and again as he feasted on her.

Opening to him, letting him all the way inside her, she whimpered, squirmed. He gave her what she was wordlessly begging for, deepening his possession, every glide against her moist silkiness, every thrust inside her fragrant deliciousness pouring fuel on his fire. Mindless with the need to devour her, to invade her, he hauled her up into his arms and strode to his bedroom with her curled up against him.

He flung himself down on the bed, taking her on top of him. She cried out as she impacted him, then again as he reversed their positions, taking her yielding, trembling body underneath him. His hands were almost rough in his haste to push her dress up and open her thighs. He groaned at the feel of her velvet firmness filling his hands. Lodging himself between her splayed smoothness, he rose on his knees to take off his jacket and shirt, tearing the latter in his haste.

Her eyes grew heavier as he exposed himself, her body undulating its plea beneath him, her voice quavering as she gasped his name between fractured breaths.

With pants still on, he slid over her again, undoing her hair's improvised confinement, driving trembling hands into her thick tresses, his gaze feverishly roaming her flushed face. That face, that essence, had taken control of his desires and fantasies from the instant he'd seen her. Now he'd take her body. He'd possess it until she wept with pleasure.

Her eyes glittered with molten gold then overflowed. He jackknifed up, gaping at her as tears spilled down her hectic cheeks in pale tracks. His thought just now had been metaphorical, but she was shedding tears for real.

She was that aroused? As aroused as he was?

Triumph and hunger raged through him like wildfire. He should be shocked at their ferocity. But he reveled in feeling out of control for the first time in his life.

"Antonio, please..."

Her tearful plea, her body buzzing beneath him with a need as brutal as his own, undid whatever sanity he had left.

He fell on her like a starving predator, his lips wrenching at hers, his tongue driving inside her as he ground himself against her.

Suddenly she was heaving beneath him, her moans becoming strangled shrieks.

It was only when her cries in his mouth turned to whimpers and her body melted limply beneath his that realization trickled through his fury of arousal.

Had she...climaxed?

Struggling to stop grinding against her, he raised himself on shaking arms, found her staring at him from slit lids, panting through swollen lips, her body nerveless.

She *had* orgasmed. Before he got her naked, before he took her, just from him emulating the act of possession. She lay beneath him, boneless, the sight and scent of her satisfaction maddening him more. Her eyes told him release had only left her hungrier, readier for his invasion.

But he'd already been jarred out of his fugue. And what he realized he'd been about to do horrified him. He would have taken her without preliminaries. Without protection. He had none here. He'd never had a woman in this house, let alone this bed, had never intended to have one here.

He could pleasure her again, but he was in too precarious a condition. If he'd lost his mind from one touch, if he continued touching her, he'd get her naked, would end up buried inside her, would ride her until she climaxed around him, wouldn't be able to stop until he spilled deep inside her womb. It would be an irretrievable step that would spoil everything.

Among all the inhuman tests he'd been exposed to and had always passed with flying colors, raising himself off her now, ending this, was the hardest thing he'd ever done.

Her hands clung weakly to him, trying to coax him back to her. He'd never resisted anything so overwhelming.

But he managed to. Rising from the bed, keeping his eyes off her so he wouldn't launch himself back at her, he strode to his dressing room and replaced the shirt he'd shredded before he strode back out to her.

His heart almost stopped when he found the bed empty. Exploding into a run, he only slowed down when he found her in the foyer, retrieving the purse she'd left on a table there.

"Liliana…"

His voice sounded as if it issued through gravel, which he felt filled his throat. Slowly, she turned to him, her face for the very first time totally unreadable. She said nothing.

"I'm sorry I pounced on you like that. It wasn't why I invited you here."

"I know. I'm the one who invited it."

Her exoneration was yet another unexpected blow that ratcheted his upheaval.

Feeling that anything he said now would make the situation worse somehow, he exhaled in frustration. "Maybe it's better if I take you home now."

Her eyes the darkest he'd seen them, she shook her head. "It's better if you don't. I'll call a cab."

He needed to argue, to convince her to let him see her home. Maybe he'd find something sane to say on the way to right the course of events that had devolved into this stilted mess. But he knew in his condition he'd only compound his mistakes.

Deciding to let her go, and to stay away from her until he got his act together, he exhaled. "I'll get Paolo to take you home." At her nod of consent, he reached for the intercom. "He lives on the premises, so he'll bring the car to the front door in a couple of minutes."

Without meeting his eyes, she again nodded, turned away and walked to the door. In seconds, she was gone.

He didn't know how long he remained rooted, staring at the door through which she'd disappeared. All he could see was how she'd looked as she'd walked away. Steady yet subdued, the energy and fire he'd always seen and felt in her every step now gone, as if something had been extinguished inside her.

Collapsing on the nearest seat, he pitched forward, burying his face in shaking hands.

What had he done?

"Won't you finally tell me what you did?"

Lili winced as Brian walked into her lab. His mood was so bright, she felt like closing her eyes to avoid its glare.

"I've been letting you get away with not telling me long enough," he said, "but after this morning, I can't wait any longer."

Yeah. Because this morning Antonio had sent a decree down his chain of command that everyone in the lab had their choice of project, whether it was one of his, their original ones or a new endeavor. Not only that, but if anyone saw fit to work on several projects simultaneously, they would be given all logistical and financial support. For scientists, who were always tied up in endless financial red tape, to be given such free rein was a dream.

"For God's sake, Lili, you have to tell me," Brian urged. "The only things I don't tell you are things you certainly don't want to hear."

She returned her eyes to her laptop to escape his merriment and curiosity. But she no longer saw the data she'd just inputted, what she believed was her first breakthrough, which had caused the first lift in her spirit in the last two weeks. The two weeks since she'd last seen Antonio.

"For the last time, Brian," she mumbled. "I didn't do anything. The man just reconsidered."

"*After* you gave him all of your mind, not just a piece of it." Brian perched his hip on her desk. "But I thought that only made him give *you* back your research. Judging from today's developments, you must have done more."

"Unless I've developed some sort of long-distance mind control, I can't see how I could have. I haven't seen the man since the day I came back to work."

The day after her magical time with Antonio came to a disastrous end.

Brian regarded her as if he was deciding whether she was telling the truth. Then his grin widened even more. "Seems you didn't have to do more. That initial dose you gave him worked like a vaccine. Its effect intensified as time went by, until he developed full immunity, or in this case, empathy with your own views."

"Botched scientific metaphor aside, it's so nice to be likened to attenuated or dead microorganisms."

"I'm likening you to the tiny busters who save lives, like you've saved ours."

Slumping back in her chair, she exhaled. "Don't exaggerate. I didn't do anything. And what lives? You were all gung ho about joining his projects."

"I myself would have worked on anything that kept me employed and serving the cause of science. But this? This is what I became a scientist hoping to do one day. This is the beginning of a life I never thought I'd be able to live. And whatever you say, I know I have you to thank for it."

"Fine. Believe whatever you want and leave me in my own version of reality, where everything is the absolute opposite of what you insinuate about my effect on Antonio Balducci."

Brain sobered when he realized she was barely reining in her agitation. "Have I put my foot in it?"

"Down to the knee joint."

Dismay flared in his eyes. "Don't tell me you've…"

"Fallen for him" went unspoken. And "been rebuffed" was also concluded.

"Man, Lili! Granted, the guy is a god, and all the women and half the men around here are swooning over him, but you of all women… I thought you'd be immune."

"Well, you thought wrong."

His gaze switched from disconcerted to solicitous in a heartbeat. "You know the last thing I want to do is step on your toes, but I know how you bottle stuff up, and how you always feel better when you talk to me about it."

"Not this time, Brian, so just drop it, okay?" His persistence had helped her once before, after her mother's death, when he'd finally gotten her to unburden herself. But knowing it wouldn't help this time, she changed the subject. "But since you're so eager to listen to me, do you have an hour? I think I'm onto something big here and I want your opinion."

Her diversion tactic worked, since scientific curiosity was the only thing that could take Brian's mind off just about anything. And for the next two hours she showed him her latest findings and he corroborated her every hope. By the time he left her, they were both certain she'd just broken through to the next level in her research.

Though this was huge, and she was beyond thrilled, that excitement didn't carry to the rest of her being. Most of her remained a prisoner to the memory of that night with Antonio.

That night, after his driver had taken her home, she'd

collapsed in bed, shaking like a leaf with both mortification and arousal.

Instead of dreaming of him, she'd stayed awake all
night, her mind filled with memories of the mindless
minutes when she'd offered herself to him, when he'd
almost taken her. His every touch and look and breath
had replayed over and over, burning her with their vivid-
ness and her humiliation. She'd been so on fire for him,
it had only taken him a few thrusts through their clothes
for her to climax.

While it had stunned her, since she'd never reached
release so easily, so violently, it had shocked him more.
Maybe even alarmed or disgusted him. For what kind
of woman would go off like that from just a few kisses
and grinds? He must have figured he'd terribly miscalculated, and the iceberg he'd thought he'd enjoy melting
had turned out to be a powder keg that would end up
blowing up in his face.

She couldn't blame him that he hadn't wanted to be
anywhere near her after that. He'd torn his gaze away
from her pleading eyes and himself from her clinging
arms, rushing to put clothes on to show her there'd be no
further intimacies. Not that she'd been about to wait for
him to come back to tell her that. She'd tried to run out
of his mansion without seeing him again. But he'd caught
up with her before she could, and though he'd tried to be
considerate, what he'd said, how he'd looked at her, had
been an even worse blow. Besides his obvious dismay
and regret, it had seemed as if he'd...pitied her.

She hadn't closed her eyes till morning after that night,
agonizing over whether to continue her earlier plan of
leaving California, or going back to the lab he'd promised she could return to on her terms.

She'd ended up going back to work. A major part of
her decision had been the hope that she'd see him again.

She'd kept envisioning scenarios of how he'd come and what she'd say, in apology, or at least in an attempt to excuse or explain her actions. Anything to take them back to where they'd been before she'd touched him and spoiled everything.

That first day back in the lab, she'd kept expecting Antonio to walk in at any moment, kept jumping at any movement or sound, imagining she'd heard his voice or caught a glimpse of him.

But he hadn't come. Not that day, not since.

With each passing day, she'd been torn more among shame, longing and despondency. Antonio had disappeared from her life as she'd known he would, only sooner and under far worse circumstances. She'd been right. All he'd needed was her capitulation. Once he'd had it, and so resoundingly, he'd lost interest. He must have even been horrified by her extreme reaction. He might have even feared he could have set himself up for a *Fatal Attraction* scenario.

It mortified her that she wouldn't be able to tell him he had nothing to worry about from her, or that she would always cherish whatever time she'd had with him. If that sounded pathetic, as it probably was, she didn't care. It was true. Being with him had been the most intense experience of her life. It pained her that what would always be a precious memory to her would be a distasteful one to him.

It also dismayed her that he'd disappeared before she could thank him. For going above and beyond in giving her everything she'd thought she'd never have, and thereby enabling her to reach the next level in her research. And he'd done that even after her accusations and suspicions and nastiness, then her reversal into a sex-starved maniac.

If she let him know through his deputies what she hoped to do, she feared he'd assign her some unsavory motivation.

Even knowing she'd never see him again, the thought of losing his admiration, his respect, hurt the most.

"Are you busy?"

That voice. *His* voice.

In the split second before she looked up, she was certain she'd find nothing there. She'd jumped at too many phantom sounds and images of him before.

But this time, her gaze didn't land on nothingness. It collided with the too-real, too-magnificent sight of Antonio Balducci.

He was really there. Peeking around her lab's door, only his head and part of his shoulders visible. As if he was ready to retreat if she said yes, she was busy.

The world dimmed, and for the first time she knew how it was possible to faint with a brutal surge of emotions. Shock, elation, trepidation and a dozen other contradictory things.

Had he come to see her? Or was he here inspecting the status of her research, thanks to his generosity? Oh, and, by the way, to put things straight with her?

"I can come back later if you prefer."

His baritone reverberated in her very being, shaking her out of her paralysis. She rose unsteadily. "No. Actually you're just the person I wanted to see."

"I am?"

"Yes, yes, I…wanted to tell you a couple of things."

Walking in and closing the door behind him, he straightened to his daunting height, this carefulness of the last time he'd faced her, almost a wariness, still permeating his body language.

Man, she'd really managed to scare him. Was he worried she might jump his bones or something?

Circling him as far away as possible, she linked her hands behind her back. "I was going to make a formal proposal and send it to you up the chain, but since you're here…"

"You don't need to do that when you need more funds or resources for your research."

"It isn't for my research." She inhaled a bolstering breath. "I've taken a comprehensive look at your…folder, and I owe you an apology. The research you wanted me to helm is right up my alley and I find it very ambitious and exciting. If I reorganize my schedule to make a timetable that would have me working on both projects simultaneously, it is completely doable, with your resources and support in place. So if you'd still like me on the project, count me in."

"Actually, I no longer want you on it."

Her heart plummeted yet again with the validation of her worst fears, that her value to him had been negated by that foolish episode. It felt like a physical blow that almost rocked her on her feet.

Struggling not to choke on the lump that expanded in her throat, she waved her hand in dismissal. "Never mind, then. It was just an idea." Then an even worse thought detonated in her mind. "If…if you don't want me here at all, I understand. You still have my resignation, and you can approve it any time you—"

"Stop." His admonition was exasperated, almost pained. "Stop jumping to conclusions about me and what I mean. I don't want you on my project because I don't want your efforts and focus divided. I want them on your own work, where you're making remarkable progress."

He did? And he knew that? How?

"But when you conclude your work successfully, if you're still interested in any of my projects, there's nothing I want more than to have the benefit of your vision and expertise." He paused, exhaled, the searing blue of his eyes suddenly darkening. "But I'm not here to talk about work."

The heart that had been expanding with his every word felt as if it shriveled again. He was here to clear that personal land mine that now existed between him and an employee he wanted to keep.

She nodded. "I understand."

"I doubt you do."

"You must want to talk about that night two weeks ago. That's the other thing I'd hoped to talk to you about. I want you to forget that embarrassing episode ever happened, and be sure nothing like that will ever happen again. Just chalk it up to pathetic inexperience and let it go at that, okay?

As if he hadn't heard a word she'd said, his gaze focused on her eyes with such intensity, she felt them misting.

"Do you know why I've stayed away these two weeks?" he asked quietly.

She forced everything in her to go still, refusing to jump to more conclusions, especially ones laden with false hopes. She'd already accepted that he'd streak through her life like a meteor, affording her a brief blaze of splendor before he disappeared. She should be thankful he'd hurtled on before he'd done more damage. She should cling to the shield of resignation, even if every cell in her body still popped with the electricity of anticipation.

When she said nothing, Antonio answered his own question. "I retreated to give you space, to reassess the damages I caused when I pursued you, besieged you, forced you out of your comfort zone and into what you might come to regret."

That was why he'd stayed away? Not for the horrible, degrading reasons she'd been torturing herself with?

"But there was another reason, too."

Her heart hit Pause, dreading his next words.

"I had to rethink everything I'd intended for this lab, to make decisions that would benefit everyone the most, by letting them resume their work or make their own choices, with my adjustments." He started walking closer, the gaze fixed on her filling with so much she couldn't bring herself to believe. "I had to prove to you, and to myself, that I can do what you can approve of, can be someone you can truly value and admire. You made me reconsider everything I do, professionally and personally."

By the time he was close enough for her to reach out and touch him again, she was ready to collapse at his feet. And that was before he made his closing statement.

"And that's why I'm here now. To tell you I want to hit a restart button with you. At your pace, on your terms."

Antonio had never dreaded anything in his life, a life filled with horrors and dangers and catastrophes. Not really.

But he dreaded Liliana's answer. He didn't know what he'd do if she rejected him.

Could he just walk away? How, when the thought of losing her sent him straight out of his ordered, controlled mind?

For two weeks he'd forced himself to stay away, until he could provide her with tangible proof of what she meant to him, how she'd changed him. That time apart from her had been almost more than he could bear. He'd spent every moment struggling not to charge after her, to carry her back to his bed and keep her there until he'd branded her, made her unable to walk away from him ever again.

But first he had to prove to her he could become a man she could trust and respect for his ability to change, to do the right thing, not only a man she could admire for his abilities or lust after for his body and the unstoppable chemistry they shared.

Waiting for her verdict as if it would decide his fate, believing it would, he struggled to keep his expression from betraying the upheaval inside him. The last thing he needed was to scare her off with the intensity of his need.

"Why?"

After every scenario he'd played out in his head, she managed to surprise him yet again with that one-word question for an answer. She neither jumped on his offer, nor made him grovel some more, nor rejected him out-right.

"You'll have to help me here, Liliana. Why what exactly?"

"Why me? Really? Now that the element of my surprise, my novelty, is gone, not to mention my resistance? When I never considered those reasons enough for you to pursue me in the first place?"

His heart contracted with an emotion he'd never both-ered with. Shame. But also wonder, that she was so attuned to him she'd sensed his early ulterior motive. This *was* his punishment for harboring those intentions, to have them resonate in her psyche, tainting her view of his motives when they no longer existed. When he now just wanted her.

Those eyes that filled his every waking and sleeping second probed his, filled with the candor and strength and vulnerability he'd become addicted to. "If you don't have specific reasons why you want me, then just tell me. Tell me what you expect from me, what you wish from being with me. I also want to know all the possible outcomes."

His head spinning, he blinked. "Outcomes?"

"Yes, like what to expect when you lose interest, how you intend to handle the eventual end of whatever we start." Her shoulders lifted in a self-conscious shrug. "I told you I can't handle uncertainty or afford upheavals."

Her scientific approach to his offer, insisting on analyzing his motives and charting a probable course for their relationship, was at once endearing and stunning. But what oppressed him was her expectation of worst-case scenarios.

"You mean you'd accept being with me even when you expect it to be a limited and finite liaison?"

She gave him such a look, as if he'd just said the most ridiculous thing, as if it was impossible for her to expect anything else, either from him or for herself.

Then she laughed, the sound mirthless. "I think anyone who enters a liaison without such expectation is just courting disaster. But I do want you so intensely that I'd take whatever is being offered, as long as I know what it is. I just need to go in knowing what to expect. That's all I ask. Total honesty."

His heart twisted with another feeling he'd never suffered from. Guilt. Total honesty was the one thing he couldn't offer her. He couldn't come clean about his initial plot to use her to get close to the Accardi family. He doubted even her pragmatic nature could forgive that. Even if it did, he feared her spontaneity with him wouldn't survive the revelation.

But he couldn't bear that she thought herself his inferior, that she expected nothing but impermanence and limitations as her due.

Itching to shake her out of those beliefs, he took her by the shoulders, groaning with the pleasure of her response, of touching her again.

"I'll say this once more and never again, Liliana. You are not only absolutely wrong in how you value yourself, but you appallingly underestimate my desire for you. I've *never* wanted anything like I want you. As for why I do, let me enlighten you. I want you because of *everything* you are. Every single thing about you fascinates me, elates me, inflames me. I adore your candor, and your wit leaves me with the bends. Your mind delights me and everything else about you, every gesture and breath and inch, makes me want to devour you. I'm the one who worries that once you come closer, it might be you who loses interest."

To say she looked incredulous was as accurate as saying she was reticent. But those eyes he'd been lost without flared with renewed life with his every word. Now their blaze made him almost give up any pretense of control.

But it was she who mattered here, and he had to make her feel secure. "All this doesn't only equalize our positions, Liliana, it makes me the supplicant. As such, I have no expectations. It's you who'll state your terms, set your parameters and every other thing you wish for in our intimacies."

Growing excitement glinted in her eyes. "What if I make outrageous demands?"

"I will welcome anything." His lips twisted as he surveyed the caring and generosity filling her expression, what he knew made up most of her being. "Though I doubt you'd ask for anything. You don't have a selfish or greedy cell in your body."

"I don't know about that, but I'd never make any demands. I want you free of obligations, for they have no place between us. I want you, and if you want me, for me, I'll be with you. Until it no longer makes you and therefore me happy." He started to object, furious that her insecurity about him hadn't been appeased, but she overrode him. "What I want to renegotiate is our professional situation. As my boss…"

He groaned his frustration at her evasion. "Will you please forget that? I'm no longer your boss. I gave you back full control over your work."

"Did you do that only to please me? To remove the obstacle of the boss/employee dynamic between us?"

He shook his head. "I do want to please you, Liliana, and remove all barriers between us, but I would have found another way to do so if I didn't believe your work held more merit than mine, given that you're so much further ahead in your research. I only attempted to force you to relinquish it initially as a demonstration of dominance. But not only am I now giving you absolute autonomy, I'm here to turn the whole lab over to you."

She staggered back. "Holy one-eighty, Antonio."

He caught her closer again, needing to convince her. "That's how you make me feel, Liliana. Like nothing I ever cared about matters anymore. Nothing but you, but us, matters to me now."

"Even so, you don't toss a two hundred-million-dollar lab at me to prove it. I told you I'm not partner material, and you want to make me director?"

"Even if you lack management skills, your scientific knowledge and your insight into your colleagues make you perfect for the job. I'll provide you with support staff who'll deal with the executive and financial issues. But in every other way, you'll make a far better boss than I can be for this place."

"Okay, time-out." She held her hands in the famous gesture. "You're clearly suffering from an extreme case of U-turn. So it's up to me to moderate you until you level out." He reached out to her hands, but she grabbed his instead. "Now listen, Antonio. I'm not taking this carte blanche or any other offer you come up with. And that's final. I only wanted to reach a common ground where both my goals and your interests could be met. I wish nothing more than to realize them both in a way that's the most beneficial for everyone."

As he looked into her earnest eyes, it was at this moment that Antonio realized something monumental.

What he felt for her.

Exactly what his brothers described they felt for their soul mates.

Love.

Seven

Love.

The word echoed in Antonio's mind as he stared at Liliana, who continued to detail how the common professional ground she was suggesting would work.

It had to be love. It *was*. This pure, limitless emotion.

But how? When he'd been in her presence only a handful of times? When he'd lived his life believing he didn't even have a heart?

But as he looked into her eyes and saw clear to her soul, saw what had delighted and spellbound him from the first, he knew.

Time was irrelevant. And he now did have a heart.

Liliana had planted one inside him.

Totally at peace with the discovery of its creation, and ecstatic about its captivity in Liliana's kind hands, he swept her in his arms and silenced her with everything that was bursting in his newly forged heart.

She melted into his kiss, not reciprocating, just yielding to him, letting him do whatever he wanted to her. That communicated how much she wanted him to possess her far more than if she'd gone wild in response.

He tore his lips from hers. "If you don't want me to take you right now, you'd better stop that."

Her long, thick lashes rose languidly, revealing passion-filled eyes that almost made him drag her down on the ground and take her there and then. "I'm not doing anything."

Pushing her back against the nearest wall, he pinned her there with his full weight, needing to imprint her with his body. "Exactly. Your surrender is sending me berserk."

"Yes, please."

"Liliana…" Her name erupted from his chest as he hitched her legs around his hips. His tongue plunged inside her open mouth, swallowing her gasps and eliciting more as he drove his hardness against her core through their clothes. "Will you come for me again?"

"Antonio…" She arched against the wall, making a fuller offer of herself.

Feeling her precious flesh burning in his hands, he quickened his cadence, the need to see her coming apart for him again riding him harder with each thrust.

"Do you know what it did to me when I felt you climaxing under me that night?" Her moans fractured, the flush staining her cheeks deepening before she buried her face in his chest. An incredulous laugh escaped him. "Are you shy?"

Suddenly she wriggled in his arms until she made him put her back on her feet, her eyes downcast. "I thought you were horrified…I thought that was why…"

A deeper wave of color surged over her face and neck. He cupped her jaw, made her look at him. "Why I stopped? I did that only because feeling you heave and tremble beneath me, realizing that I aroused you so much I drove you to orgasm even before taking you, snapped my control for the first time in my life."

She regarded him with a mixture of self-consciousness and disbelief. "You didn't seem out of control at all."

"It must be my surgeon facade. But if I'd remained near you one more minute, I would have taken you. Without protection. And I knew you'd let me."

Her eyes widened in realization and admission, proving he'd been right. She *would* have let him. She wanted him inside her without barriers, branding her with his pleasure. As he would, soon.

"I had to get away from you since I had no more control and your every touch and breath and glance had me at breaking point."

A keen escaped her as she crushed herself to him, silently demanding he stop holding back.

Unable to even contemplate it anymore, he pressed her to the wall again. He was devouring her whimpers, undulating feverishly against her when a one-note buzz jolted through them both.

His phone. The line he kept for his brothers.

Dammit.

Setting her down but unable to stop caressing her, he gestured an apology as he pulled the phone out.

It was an integral part of their brotherhood's pact, to answer a call from a brother at once. They'd depended on one another to survive, then to escape, then to conquer the world. A brother's call trumped everything. They never called one another on those special lines unless it was something serious. As the group's doctor, he'd gotten many of those calls.

Then came the last couple of years. Since then he'd gotten calls that were serious only in his brothers' eyes. After all, they considered any twinge their wives or children suffered the end of the world.

But this was Ivan. He wasn't married and would never be if all remained right with the world. Ivan had never called him on this line. Not once.

His heart thudding in mounting trepidation, he pushed the answer button. "Ivan?"

"Tonio, I'm landing in LA in half an hour. I need you and your best surgical team ready. Code Whiteout."

Code Whiteout meant he needed Antonio's secret surgical facility, where he had a special team on standby and where he treated injuries they needed kept below law enforcement's radar.

He gritted his teeth at the agitation he felt cracking his best friend's usual Siberian composure. "Tell me."

"A…friend and his sister. They were gunned down. I have a team stabilizing them. I need you to put them back together."

"I'll meet you there."

Ivan ended the call without another word. Antonio turned to Liliana, found she'd walked away to give him privacy.

He rushed after her, caught her in a ferocious hug. "I have to go, *mi amore*. Emergency surgery."

She almost jumped at his endearment, her eyes flooding with such exquisite delight. "Of course."

"Do you know how I hate leaving you now?"

"If it's as much as I hate you leaving, I pity you fiercely." Her smile wobbled as she caressed his cheek. "But duty calls. To both of us. I'd better get back to work before the bright ideas I was working on evaporate." He hugged her again as if afraid *she* somehow would. Seeming to read his paranoia right, she grinned. "I'll be right here when you're done."

"From the preliminary report, I don't foresee being done for the next twelve hours. If that."

"Then I'll see you whenever you can see me." She brushed his hair back, her touch soothing and bolstering.

He got out his keys, pressed them into her hand. "I'll text you my security codes and Paolo's number. He'll pick you up from your house after you get what you need. I want you there when I get home."

Her eyes made him this promise, and so many more, all of which he knew she'd keep no matter what. Then she stood on tiptoes and kissed him, giving him a glimpse of the ecstasy they'd share.

Before he grabbed her again, she stepped out of his arms, turned him around and marched him to the door. "The sooner you're gone, the sooner you'll be back to me."

As he stepped outside her lab, his heart lurched. Leaving her felt like leaving behind a vital part of himself.

"I'll be home as soon as I can."

"Oh, no, you're not rushing a surgery on my account. I'll be there no matter how late you are. And if you're not home by tomorrow morning, you know where to find me. Now, shoo."

At her grin, he groaned and turned away, forcing himself not to look back. He'd be late if he did, and Ivan would kill him. He'd do his job then rush home to her.

The anticipation kept him flying high all the way to his secret facility on the fringes of LA. It was only when he was entering it that he realized something.

When he'd given Liliana his keys, he'd been asking her to move in with him. He'd texted her nonstop on the way, but from her answers it was clear she thought he wanted her there only tonight. Even thinking that, she'd taken the keys happily. It pained him all over again that she didn't have any expectations, was truly content with anything he offered.

It made him wonder how such unconditional passion

was possible, and how he of all people was on its receiving end.

But even if he didn't deserve it yet, he would.

He would deserve *her*.

It was 2:00 a.m. by the time he finished the surgeries.

It would have been much longer if he'd had to perform trauma repair and reconstruction on both patients. But by the time he had them on his table, he'd known one of them would not make it. Ivan's friend. The sister was critical but could survive with a liver transplant. Her brother was a tissue match for her and Antonio could harvest his liver, which had been one of the few things remaining intact in him. Ivan, who'd been watching everything in the gallery, had told him to do *anything* to save her. Which he had.

Letting his team take her to the ICU now, he tore his bloody scrubs off and stepped out of the OR. Ivan was right at the door, looking like he'd go on a rampage at any moment.

"Sorry about your...friend." Antonio wouldn't ask for details. Ivan would tell him if he wanted him to know. "I trust you know who did this to them?"

Ivan's usually forbidding face turned positively demonic. "They're already dead."

That was quick, even for Ivan. But then, no one could hide from him. Ivan had always traced the untraceable. But being the lord of the cyber world wasn't where his talents ended. His business rivals called him Ivan the Terrible, unsuspecting that Ivan was literally lethal. He was as accomplished an assassin as any of their other brothers.

"She will be fine, won't she?"

Antonio exhaled, rubbing his stiff neck. Ten hours of operating on Ivan's mystery woman had been extra grueling, mostly because of Ivan's volcanic agitation. Antonio did everything he could for all his patients, but when one of his brothers was involved, the stakes were almost unmanageable. Something he didn't relish while having a human life under his scalpel.

"She will be. But even after I discharge her, it'll be a long road to recovery. Does she have anyone to take care of her?"

"She has me."

Antonio went still. Coming from Ivan, this was major.

It *could* be duty driving him, or a debt he owed his dead friend. But Antonio felt this went far beyond that. Though Ivan had never intimated that he'd ever cared for a woman, Antonio felt this one was important to him. Very important. In a way no woman had ever been.

This was either a relationship Ivan had chosen not to tell him about, or it was a new development, as intense and life-changing as his situation with Liliana.

And if this weren't such a grim occasion, Antonio would have told him about her, would have joked about the brothers falling like dominoes one after the other.

But if Ivan felt about this woman like Antonio did for Liliana, what had happened to her, what was still ahead of her, must be killing him. While he had so much joy to look forward to with Liliana starting tonight, Ivan could only watch the woman he cared about struggle for her life.

Feeling guilty that he was the happiest he'd ever been while Ivan suffered his worst pain, Antonio grabbed him by the shoulders. "She *will* be fine, Ivan. She's strong, and you brought her to me in the best condition possible. I believe her brother was lost at the scene, and it was only your efforts that kept his systems going till you got him here. It's the only reason his organs were viable, making the transplant possible. It was you who saved her."

Ivan avoided his eye, kept his downcast under the blackest frown Antonio had ever seen as he turned away. But not before Antonio saw what felt like a blow to the solar plexus. His iceberg of a friend's eyes filling with tears.

Knowing Ivan wouldn't want him to acknowledge his upheaval, he followed him in silence to the ICU's observation area.

He stood behind him, felt agony radiating off him as he watched his mystery woman being hooked to monitors and drips.

"I'm a phone call away, Ivan."

Back rigid, breathing strident, Ivan only nodded.

Knowing he could do no more for now, Antonio exhaled at the unaccustomed feeling of helplessness and walked away.

An hour later, Antonio entered his mansion. It was dim and quiet. But he knew Liliana was there. She'd texted him, and so had Paolo the moment she'd gone inside safely.

He walked through the foyer into the great room and found her there on the couch, her hair streaming off its edge in a cascade of curls. She was sound asleep.

He approached her soundlessly and looked down at her. With his best friend's ordeal reverberating in his being, seeing her there, whole and irreplaceable, had a storm of emotions raging inside him. He wanted to wake her up, lose himself inside her, hide her within himself. And none of it was about lust. It was about passion and protection. Tenderness and togetherness. And everything he'd never shared with or offered another human being.

Unable to keep away anymore, he bent to pick her up. The moment he touched her, she opened her eyes. They penetrated him to his very recesses with their instant welcome. As she tried to sit up, he scooped her up and pressed her head to his shoulder.

"Shh, *cuore mio*, don't wake up."

She nestled deeper into his hold, her lips moving against

his thundering heart as she spoke. "I was just dreaming of you…as usual."

"Then continue dreaming, *mi amore*."

He carried her to his bed, their bed now, wondering again that he was using Italian.

He'd learned the language in The Organization, perfecting it before he had English. They always taught every child his mother tongue, so they'd use him in missions involving his country or countrymen. But he'd never spoken it outside of those times.

Liliana made him speak it. He wanted to lavish on her the passionate endearments unique to the language he should have grown up speaking. Somehow, only they felt right to express what he felt for her.

Reaching his bed, he placed her lovingly on it before remotely parting the drapes, letting the moonlight in. He started to undress her, and she stirred again. She caught his hands, embarrassment staining her cheeks in the silver light.

He kissed her, pushed her back gently, crooning encouragement and praise to her as his hands roamed her body, and she melted back again, letting him do anything he pleased. And it did please him, beyond words, to get rid of every barrier, to finally see that body that had inflamed his though it had always been obscured.

And she was divine. Smooth and strong and sinuous, in the exact proportions he'd just discovered translated into his personal definition of perfection.

She watched him throughout, hanging on his reactions. He didn't leave it to her deductions. He told her exactly what he thought. Then he started undressing himself, reveling in the awed, voracious look that possessed her face. If there was ever a reward for the years he'd spent training and maintaining his physique, it was *that* look. He was already addicted to it. Then he removed the last of his clothing, letting her see just how hard her beauty and her hunger made him.

At the sight of his erection, she gasped and sank back deeper in the bed, as if she already felt it invading her, pinning her to the mattress. She licked her lips, those lips he wanted nothing more than to feel around his hardness.

But that would come later. Now he needed to reassure himself that she was safe with him. That she was his to cherish, to protect.

Getting into bed beside her, he pulled her into his burning body. He groaned in unison with her long moan, aching and relieved, as their flesh touched without barriers for the first time. Then, gradually, he felt her tension dissipate in the serenity of deep sleep.

He watched her, at peace in his arms, for as long as he could, before he too succumbed. To the first true rest of his life.

He woke up to unknown yet breathtaking sensations. Silk and velvet sweeping all over his body.

Liliana was trailing her hands and hair and lips over him, caressing and kissing and delighting in him.

The light beyond his closed lids said it was around sunset. He'd never slept that long. Nor had he ever slept with anyone present except his brothers. He'd certainly never fallen asleep with a woman in the same bed. Not once in his life.

He kept his eyes closed for as long as he could bear, to savor her worshipping, his heart drumming to a slow, hungry rhythm.

Then he couldn't take it anymore. In the same second he opened his eyes, he reached for her, swept her around and beneath him. This time, there would be no stopping him.

"Antonio."

The way she made his name sound like an aching plea. For him. For everything with him.

He took her lips. A thousand volts crackled between them, unleashing everything inside him in a tidal wave.

Maddened by the immediacy of her surrender, he captured her lower lip in a growling bite, stilling its tremors, attempting to moderate his passion. But she made it impossible when she parted her lips wider for his invasion, and her taste inundated him.

Such unimaginable sweetness. And the perfume of her breath, the sensory overload of her feel. Everything about her was a hallucinogen that pounded through his system, snapping the tethers of his sanity.

Her whimpers urged him to intensify his possession. His hands shook with urgency as he wrapped her legs around his hips, rose to revel in the overpowering sight she made trembling in his arms.

"Tell me, *mi amore*. Tell me you need me to take you."

Her answer was only squeezing her eyes in languorous acquiescence.

"I will take everything you have, Liliana, devour everything you are and give you all of me. Is this what you want? What you need? Now? And from now on?"

Lili heard Antonio as if from the depths of a dream.

Everything that had happened since he'd come to her yesterday making his offer of himself, on her terms, felt like one.

But in her wildest fantasies, she wouldn't have dared hope for Antonio to feel the same sweeping desire for her, or to succumb to it, let alone as quickly as she had.

But he did. He had. And once again he was demanding her confession and consent. He was holding back to make certain she craved his invasion and sanctioned his ferocity.

Oh, how she did. Even if the power of his dominance,

the starkness of his lust, staggered her. She might have come to his mansion, let him take her to his bed, might have been so bold as to wake the sleeping tiger, but now as she lay beneath him, waiting to be devoured, a storm of agitated desire overwhelmed her.

Her heart plunged into arrhythmia and she felt as if her every cell swelled, screamed for his possession.

Almost swooning with need, she gazed up at him as he loomed above her, the fiery palette of the horizon framing his magnificent body, setting his beauty ablaze. His eyes looked filled with tempests, precariously checked. He was giving her one last chance to dictate the terms of her surrender before he devastated her.

Feeling she'd die if he didn't she told him, "Take all of me, give me your all. Do everything to me, Antonio...*everything*. I need it all."

Raking her body in fierce greed, he bared his teeth on a soft snarl as he cupped her breasts in hands that trembled, kneaded them as if they were the most amazing things he'd ever felt. Then he bent and took one nipple in the damp furnace of his mouth, squeezing a shriek out of her. She unraveled with every nip and suck, each with the exact pressure and intensity to extract maximum pleasure. He layered sensation upon sensation until she felt inundated.

She was shaking out of control when he slid down her body, painting her with caresses and licks until he stilled an inch from her core, his breath on her making her feel she'd spontaneously combust.

He lit her fuse when he spoke, his voice a ragged, bass growl. *"Perfetto, bellezza, magnifica."*

As if everything about him weren't overkill already, he had to go speak Italian. It made her writhe.

"Antonio, *please*..."

"Si, amore, I will please you...always and forever."

He pressed his face to her thighs, his lips opening over

her quivering flesh like a starving man who didn't know where to start his feast. Her fingers convulsed in his silky hair, pressed him to her flesh, unable to handle the stimulation, yet needing even more.

He dragged a hand between her thighs, electrifying her as the heel of his thumb brushed open her outer lips. Her undulations became feverish, her pleas a litany till he dipped a finger between her molten lips, stopping at her entrance.

"I dreamed of you like this from that first day, open to me, letting me possess and pleasure you."

He spread her legs, placed them over his shoulders, opening her core to him fully. Her moans became keens, sharpening, gasping.

He inhaled her, rumbling like a lion at the scent of his female in heat, as she was. He blew a gust of sensation over the knot where her nerves gathered. Her hips rose to him, a plea escaping her lips. It became a shriek when he finally, slowly, slid a finger inside her and she came, pleasure slamming through her in desperate surges.

He'd again made her climax with one touch.

Among the aftershocks, she felt his finger inside her, pumping, beckoning at her inner trigger. Her gasp tore through her lungs as his tongue joined in, circling her bud. Each glide and graze and pull and thrust made her need ignite again as if she hadn't just had the most intense orgasm of her life.

Soon she was sobbing, bucking again, opening herself fully to his double assault until he had her quaking and screaming with an even more violent release.

She tumbled from the explosive peak, drained, stupefied.

From the depth of drugged satiation, her heavy gaze sought his in the receding sunset. His eyes glowed azure, heavy with hunger and satisfaction.

"From now on you're on my menu every single day," he whispered. "I'm already addicted to your taste and your pleasure."

Something squeezed inside her until it became almost painful. It flabbergasted her to recognize it as an even fiercer arousal. Her satisfaction had lasted a minute and now she was even hungrier. No, she felt something else she'd never felt before. Empty. As if a void inside her was growing, demanding to be filled. By him. Only ever him.

"Don't indulge your addiction now." She barely recognized her voice, sultry with hunger, hoarse from her cries. "If you don't give me yourself right now, I might implode."

All lightness drained from his eyes as he squeezed her mound possessively, the ferocious conqueror flaring back to life. "And you will have me. I'll ride you to ecstasy until you can't beg for more."

His sensual threat filled her with nervous anticipation. Her heart went haywire as he slid back up over her, sowed kisses over her from her mound to her face, before he withdrew to look down at her.

His exhalation was ragged. "Do you realize how incredible you are?" As she mumbled something between dismissal and embarrassment, he persisted. "Don't you *see* how incredible I find you?"

He rose above her, displaying the full measure of his sculpted perfection. She struggled to her elbows, her mouth watering, her hands stinging, with the need to explore him, revel in him.

But he wasn't inviting her to witness or examine his splendor, but demonstrating her effect on him. Glimpsing his manhood in the semidarkness last night had filled her sleep with sexual torment. It was why she hadn't been able to keep her hands off him when she'd woken up, though she hadn't dared remove the sheet he tented even in sleep.

Now she forced her gaze down…and was again awestruck at the size and beauty of him.

What if she couldn't accommodate him? Please him?

His muscles bunched as he reached down to the floor, picked up the pants he'd discarded and produced a foil packet. He was ready this time. Last time he hadn't been, which meant he didn't have women here. That was such a momentous realization, it made this even more incredible than it already was.

Then holding her eyes in such promise, he tore the packet open.

She almost came again just watching him sheath himself.

"Now I take you, *mi amore*. And you take me."

Though she shook with agitation, she whimpered, "Yes…yes, please."

She received him in trembling arms as he came down over her. She cried out at how her softness cushioned his hardness.

Perfect. No, sublime.

Pushing her legs wider apart, his eyes solicitous, tempestuous, he bathed himself in her readiness in slow strokes from bud to opening, driving her to desperation before he growled and finally sank inside her in one long, fierce thrust.

A red-hot lance of pain had the world flickering out for long moments, squeezing a cry from her very depths, before other sensations surged back in a rush, none she'd ever felt before. Fullness, completion.

Her eyes fluttered open to find him turned to stone on top of her, his eyes wild with worry.

"You're a… You were a… It's your first time!"

Quivering inside and out, the last thing she wanted was to talk, her mind unraveling with the feel of him filling her. But she had to answer his strangled exclamation. "You do remember me saying I was pathetically inexperienced, don't you?"

His distress ebbed, tenderness replacing it. "Oh, yes, I do. *Dio mio*, you're a surprise a second. Make that a shock a second. I didn't think you meant...*that*."

"What else did you think I meant?"

"I didn't think. I basically *can't* think around you."

Then he started withdrawing from her depths, making her feel he was turning her inside out.

"No!" She clung to him with her arms and legs, tried to drag him back inside her. "Don't go. Don't stop."

Throwing his head back, he squeezed his eyes. "I'm only trying not to lose my mind here, *mi amore*, in consideration of your...state of inexperience. Don't make it impossible." He opened his eyes. "I'd only stop if you wanted me to."

Emptiness threatening to engulf her, she thrust her hips upward, impaling herself on his massive girth, uncaring about the chafing pain, even needing it. "I'd die if you stopped."

His groan was pained, as if she'd hurt him, too. "Stopping would probably finish me, as well. For real."

She thrust up again, crying out as he stretched her, the sensation making her delirious.

His hand combed through her hair, dragged her down by its tether to the mattress, pinning her there. Her heart shook her like an earthquake as she crushed herself against him. "Don't hold back. I love the way you feel inside me. I *love* it. Fill me, hurt me until you make it better."

"*Si, amore*, I'll make it so much better." He cupped her hips in both hands, tilted them into a cradle for his own, then slowly thrust inside her to the hilt.

It was beyond overwhelming, being full of him. The reality, the meaning and carnality of it, rocked her essence.

He withdrew again, and she cried out at the unbearable

loss, urged him to sink back into her. He resisted her pleas, taking his time, resting at her entrance before he thrust back inside her. Then again, and again. Slow, measured, making her cry out hot gusts of passion and open herself wider with every plunge.

Holding her gaze, he watched her intently, avidly, adjusting his movements to her every moan and grimace, waiting for pleasure to fully submerge the pain. He kept her at a fever pitch, caressing her all over, sucking her breasts, draining her lips, raining wonder over her. "*Perfetto, amore*, inside and out. Everything about you is perfect."

Her body soon rewarded his patience and expertise. It gushed readiness and pleasure over him, demanding everything he could give her.

"Antonio, I need everything now, please."

"*Si, bellezza*, everything." His groan reverberated in her mouth as he drove his tongue inside her to his plunging rhythm, quickening both.

Everything within her tightened unbearably, her depths rippling around him, reaching for that elusive something, something way beyond orgasm, nothing she'd ever attained, but that she felt she'd perish if she didn't have now.

No longer coherent, she begged him, over and over. "Please, Antonio, please."

But he understood, knew she couldn't bear the buildup anymore. "*Si, amore, ora.* Now I give you all the pleasure this divine body of yours can withstand."

Tilting her up toward him, he hammered inside her with a force and cadence that rattled the whole world, dismantled her every cell. He breached her to her womb on each plunge until he detonated the coil of desperation in her deepest recess.

Convulsions tore through her, clamping her inner muscles around him as her insides splintered with pleasure too agonizing to register, then to bear, then to bear having it end.

But it didn't end. It went on and on as he gave her more and more, until finally she cried out with his each jarring thrust.

Then came a moment she'd replay in her memory forever. The sight of him as he climaxed inside her.

Her orgasm intensified as he threw his head back to bellow his own pleasure. He fed her convulsions with his, his release so fierce she felt it through the barrier, making her sob with the need to feel its hot surges filling her.

Whimpering as he continued to move within her, completing her pleasure, her domination, she was helpless to do anything but let the enormity of his first possession drag her into oblivion.

Eight

An eternity later, Lili surged back into her body, realizing what had brought her back. Antonio was moving, starting to leave her body.

Unable to bear separation, she clung to him. He pressed soothing kisses to her eyes and lips, murmuring reassurance in that voice that strummed everything in her as he swept her around, careful to remain inside her. Then she was lying on top of him, satiated in ways she couldn't have imagined, reverberating with the magnitude of the experience and in perfect peace for the first time in her life.

When her heart stopped thundering enough to let her breathe, she raised a wobbling head. "Is it…always like that?"

His eyes looked as dazed as she felt, and his lips twitched. "It's never been like that for me. Everything with you is always a first."

"You're telling me that's not why people make such a

fuss about sex? Because it's that…that…" No description could do what had happened between them justice.

"In my experience, 'sex' has absolutely nothing in common with what we just had. This was…magic."

Her body began to throb all over again. "It was for me."

"You have nothing to compare it to, but I do, so I know how magical it was, and what made it so." Before she could infer the meaning of his confession he added, "It's because I love you."

She bolted upright, gaping down at him.

He started withdrawing from her depths carefully as he sat up, too. In spite of her paralysis, her moan echoed his groan at the burn of separation. Her gaze remained meshed with his as he looked at her as if she were the one thing he lived for.

"I realized it yesterday. That all those overwhelming feelings I feel for you are love."

She collapsed on the bed in a daze, could do nothing but watch him as he rose to discard the condom. Then he came back to tower over her, godlike, still fully engorged, a frown of uncertainty creeping over his face.

"I can see this comes as a shock."

Her heart stumbling, eyes stinging, she could only choke, "That's the understatement of our era."

"Is it a good or bad shock?"

He seemed actually worried. Very worried. *Really?*

It was the only thing she could say out loud. "Are you for real? Is that even a question?"

His shoulders rose and fell. "I've learned to never assume anything with you. You never react in any way I expect. I also realize this could seem too quick—"

"You think?" She felt caught in a hurricane of disbelief and jubilation that uprooted her very existence. "It's been less than a week."

"It's been *three* weeks."

"Two of which you didn't even see me."

"Because I was on a mission to be worthy of you and your trust and respect. And I did see you. I was watching you."

Her mouth dropped open. "You were?"

His grin was sheepish. "I practically stalked you. At home, at work. Before you ask how, I...have my ways."

She struggled up to her elbow, incredulousness mushrooming inside her. "I'm sure you have. But even so..."

Lowering himself to the bed, he stretched out beside her, gathering her along his hot, hard body. "I've always made life-and-death decisions in seconds. Taking three weeks to conclude that I love you is a glacial pace for me. I took that long only because the decision to love you for the rest of my life is way more weighty than any life-and-death issue I've ever dealt with."

She shook her head. How could all this be happening?

His large hand cupped her head. "Do you know why I came back to you when I did?"

"Because you completed that quest you thought would make you worthy of me?"

"You think it took me two whole weeks to do that? Everything was in place in two days."

She blinked dazedly. "So why?"

"I was waiting for you."

"To do what? Seek you out?"

"No, to reach your breakthrough. I knew you were close when I first acquired the lab, and that when you used the resources I put at your disposal, you'd no doubt reach it. I didn't want to come back before you did. I wanted you to have this achievement you so deserve, before I distracted the hell out of you."

That was tremendous. Unbelievable. But... "If you came the next day and explained that I didn't put you off and you didn't fear I'd boil your rabbit, I wouldn't have agonized over you with every breath. I might have even reached that breakthrough sooner."

His frown was spectacular. "Dammit. Everything I do because of you or for you backfires right in my face."

She caressed his cheek placatingly. "With an end result that's far better than any plan could have projected. Look at where I am now with my work, how ecstatic everyone is that you bought the lab. Look at me lying here with you, after you've given me absolute pleasure and so much more I never dreamed I'd have, and are now telling me that you… you…" A strangled cry escaped her as she buried her face into his chest, tears pouring from the depths of her soul. "This is…you are…too much. Way more than my heart can withstand or contain."

"You are impossible for my heart to withstand or contain, too. What I feel for you is so intense, I feel I would go mad if you don't reciprocate."

"Oh God, I do, Antonio. I *love* you. I think from the first moment I saw you. But I never thought you could love me back."

"You captured me from that first moment, too. I know myself, and I can promise you one thing—I'll love you more every day. I only hope you never think I love you too much."

She surged into him, shaking, tears flowing, unable to talk or breathe anymore. Her heart was overflowing. He soothed her, caressed her all over, sucking her lips, her nipples, lavishing the most amazing endearments and praise on her until she wrapped herself around him, undulated against him.

"Take me again, Antonio."

His laugh was distressed as he unclasped her thighs from around his waist. "You might think you're ready for another round, but trust me, you're not." He laid her back gently, his gaze scorching her all over before returning to her eyes, filled such sensual indulgence her core cramped with need. "So...never before, eh?"

Feeling free to show him everything in her heart and how wanton he made her, she rubbed her nipples against his rock-hard chest. "Apart from...uh...self-help, no. Why bother, when it wasn't you?"

His gaze went supernova as he crushed her to him, then her lips beneath his.

When he let her breathe again, she felt self-conscious again. "So you're not wondering how I reached this age without having sex? You don't find it..."

"Pathetic?" he repeated her earlier description of her inexperience. "What's pathetic is how ferociously glad I am that you didn't." He pressed into her, his arousal undiminished, his body buzzing with vitality and dominance and lust. "And I don't find it strange at all, now that I know you. You don't do anything unless it satisfies your meticulous, exacting mind, and I am only proud and grateful I'm the one who does. After you made me work my ass off for it, of course."

He understood. And appreciated. Her heart swelled with thankfulness, even as it still quaked with the enormity of knowing he loved her back.

She caressed his hewn cheek, letting him see everything inside her. "I never wanted anyone, never considered anyone worth the trouble. But even when I thought you were unattainable and knew you would be trouble of unimaginable magnitude, I wanted you. I craved you, in any way, for any length of time, no matter the price. Or I thought I craved you. After this...cataclysm, I'm addicted to you."

After another smothering, devouring kiss, he withdrew. "It's merciful you are, since I'm beyond addicted to you. It's also lifesaving for those men you didn't bother with. If you had, I would have gone hunting them."

She burst out laughing. "Now I've got an image emblazoned forever in my mind. You in a loincloth, chasing poor, inferior men, clubbing them over the head and throwing them in a pile."

His smile was predatory. "*Si, amore*, laugh at the caveman your love has made of me."

Arching with an unbearable surge of delight and desire, she opened for his erection, needing him back inside her. "Go caveman all over me, please."

His pupils flared in warning. "I'm barely holding him back, so behave. You're too sore now."

"But I want you to let him loose. Make me almost die of pleasure again, Antonio."

Groaning as if in pain, he thrust against her. "From the first time you cut me up with that tongue of yours, I knew. That under the guise of the prim, contentious scientist there was a woman I wanted desperately. But even I wasn't ambitious enough to hope I'd find this, the most perfect, uninhibited sex goddess. You almost killed me with pleasure, too."

"Then take us to the edge of mortality again, *please*."

"Command me, *amore*. You only have to breathe, to just be, and I would literally die for you."

Before her mind could wrap around those earthshaking words, he rose over her, opened her wide around his hips and slid his hardness between the molten lips of her core. He nudged her nub and the world vanished in a burst of pleasure.

It came so quickly, a boil in her blood, a tightening in depths that now knew exactly how to unfurl and undo her. She opened herself for him, knowing he would only pleasure her this way, undulating faster against him until another orgasm, different yet still magnificent, tore through her.

He pinned her down as she came, gliding his shaft against her quivering flesh in the exact pressure and rhythm to drain her of every spark her body needed to discharge.

After she slumped in quivering fulfillment, he rose between her spread legs and pumped himself to a roaring climax.

Watching him take his pleasure over her trembling body, the body he now owned, was mesmerizing. It was the most flagrantly erotic sight she'd ever witnessed, and the most profoundly fulfilling emotion she'd ever felt.

Pulling her to his body, he mingled their sweat and pleasure and heartbeats, surrounding her in his love and cherishing, dragging her into a realm of safety and contentment.

When next she woke up, it was to Antonio's caresses.

He was wiping her down with something wet and warm. Moaning, she opened her eyes to find him bent over her in dim, golden light, a being out of a fable, cosseting and worshipping her. Joy surged on a tremulous smile as she sought his eyes, only for it to be aborted at the sight of the disturbed expression in their depths.

That had her scrambling up, her heart shedding its languor, starting to drum painfully. "What's wrong, Antonio?"

He exhaled, continued to rub her stomach. "I was watching you sleeping so trustingly in my arms...and I kept wondering how you feel the same for me. Or how you'd continue to."

She stopped his hand. "Where is this coming from?"

Extricating his hand from her grip, he threw the hand towel aside squeezed his eyes shut briefly. "Apart from my...partners, I never had any relationship of any sort with anyone."

This was all? She poked her elbow in his side, inviting him to grin back at her. "Same here."

"You're nowhere near the same, *mi amore*."

"Of course I'm not. You're unique."

He shook his head. "It's you who are. While having more money and power than almost anyone doesn't mean I'm anywhere near your level."

"I already told you I don't factor your money and power in your uniqueness. The man you are beneath the trappings, the force of nature who achieved such success, who saves lives and puts bodies back together like no one else can, who turns everything he touches into the best it can be…that's the man I love."

"*Dio mio, dea mia.* You're far more than I ever imagined anyone could be. You're far better than I deserve."

She scrambled up to her knees, caught his hot face in trembling hands. "Why, my love? Why do you feel that way? When you said you feared I'd be the one to lose interest, I thought you were being gallant. But you meant it, didn't you?"

He nodded. "It scares me like nothing has before, that one day you'll look inside me and hate what you see."

This was more serious than she'd first imagined. And it needed to be resolved, at once.

She sat back on her heels, feeling it was the most natural thing to be naked with him in every sense of the word.

"When you told me you grew up without your father, too, I thought I saw scars beyond your perfect, placid facade and I hoped they'd been long healed. But now I feel this goes far deeper than growing up fatherless like me, that you suffered way more hardships and injustices and abuse than anything I can imagine. And it makes me even more proud of you and in awe of what you attained in spite of it all."

"What if you're right, and there's way more to me that you can dream of in your worst nightmares? What if it's so terrible that if you knew, it would send you away screaming?"

"You're not hypothesizing, are you? You're really afraid I can't handle the truth." His eyes went bleak, overwhelming her with the need to unburden him. She pressed her hands to his heart, needing to absorb his pain. "This damage I feel inside you…it goes beyond a physical or psychological ordeal. You've…done things. Ugly things." His gaze faltered, and it felt as if his last reluctance gave way, letting her plunge deep. And she felt she was reading everything inside him, dragging out every festering darkness. Her voice shook as she put what she saw into words. "You were involved in…violence. You used your skills in cold-blooded and lethal ways. Even to…kill."

She bated her breath as his eyes widened, stunned.

Then all the fire that had ever been there was extinguished and he only said, "Yes."

Ever since Antonio had realized he wanted Liliana, he'd broken out in cold sweat just thinking how it would hurt her if she ever learned she'd initially been a tool in his plan of revenge, even if he hadn't and would never act on it.

Though he couldn't come clean about it, ever, he needed to be honest with her any other way he could. He'd already started by opening up about his feelings. Now he needed to go further, all the way, and open up about himself.

His surface was as perfect and placid as she'd said. But he was anything but inside. Not even his brothers knew of the wreckage inside him. But *she'd* seen it. She'd said it made her proud of him that he'd become what he was in spite of what he'd been through. But though she'd somehow seen what no one else had even guessed at, she still couldn't even guess at the specifics.

What if he told her all the things he'd done as a slave of The Organization, what he'd had to do to gain his freedom, and it horrified her? What if she thought him too damaged, beyond redemption, and ran for her life?

But he owed her the whole truth. He'd keep from her only what might hurt her feelings or damage her trust in him. What didn't apply to them anymore anyway, and never would.

More than anything he wanted to make her promise she'd never leave him no matter what she learned, but he couldn't do that. She'd give him her pledge, and she'd keep it, even if she hated it and him. She was that noble, that kind. No, she had to have total freedom to act in her own best interests. Even if it meant leaving him behind. Even if he couldn't survive without her.

Needing to put some distance between them so he wouldn't weaken, he pulled away from her, rose to fetch his pants.

As he came back to stand over her, she pulled the sheet over herself, as if she feared she couldn't face whatever he'd say in the vulnerability of nakedness. It made him hate himself more for causing her even a moment's uncertainty or anxiety.

Holding her suddenly fragile gaze, praying she wouldn't end up hating him, he said, "Though I'd give anything for you not to know, you need to know. What I am, what I've done. I'll abide by whatever decision you make once you know everything."

And he exposed all the horrors of his past, what not even his brothers knew. The only thing he left out was the identity of the family who'd discarded him.

All through his confession, what most agonized him were the brutal emotions that ravaged her, from shock to horror to denial to desolation. He couldn't stop to analyze each one so he could go on.

When he was done, he stood before her, unable to believe he'd finally unburdened himself, shaking with the discharge of a lifetime of torment and rage that he'd suppressed under layers of steely discipline. But what truly shook him was dreading the reason behind her weeping.

Before he could bring himself to ask, she scrambled off the bed and launched herself at him so explosively, she made him stumble and fall.

He barely caught himself before he crashed flat on the ground, cushioning her on top of him as she rained copious tears and frenzied kisses all over him. She sobbed so hard he was terrified she'd do herself real damage.

He frantically tried to soothe her. "*Mi amore*, please, nothing is worth your tears. I beg you, don't cry."

She shook her head and cried harder, but he finally understood what she was reiterating in her incoherent sobbing.

"My love, my love, I'm sorry, I'm so sorry, so sorry…"
This was all for him.

His one-of-a-kind, magnanimous firecracker was breaking her own heart on his behalf.

He crushed her to him, trying to defuse her upheaval. "*Mi amore*, it's all in the past. I just needed you to know."

She struggled out of his hold and rose above him, her eyes reddened, her lips quaking. "And I'd give anything, *everything*, if I could undo it all, make you un-suffer every single second."

He caught her face, stilled its shuddering. "You have. Just telling you, just that it didn't matter to you, worked like an antidote to the poison I had in my system. I can now leave it all behind where it can't touch me, or us, again. Just loving you erases it all, makes up for it a hundred times over."

Her sobs lessened as he talked, stroked her hair, pressed her to his chest.

With her upheaval fading, she spoke against his flesh. "You know what's driving me insane right now? Besides being unable to go after those who hurt you and making them suffer a far worse hell than the one they put you through? It's that I had such a ridiculously easy life compared to you. I can't even share your ordeals except in my imagination. And I *hate* it!"

He went still beneath her. His heart had expanded until he wondered if it would burst. Not a bad way to go, he thought. If he didn't want to live forever. To be with Liliana.

"*Mi amore, sposami.* Marry me."

His words echoed in absolute silence.

They'd both stopped breathing. The very world stopped turning.

Then both their chests emptied on ragged moans as she raised an unsteady head to look down at him, flabbergasted.

And everything poured out of him. "I never had a heart, but you created one inside me. A heart that was made to love you, that can't survive without you. So if you want me alive, you'll have to say yes."

She burst into tears again. "God, Antonio, yes...*yes*. But..."

"No buts."

"I was just going to say—but I think you should slow down, take more time to think about this. After you do—"

His lips silenced hers. "I can't slow down, and I won't think about it. I want nothing else but you. I now realize everything in my life has been leading up to this. This moment. This union. You." He took her in another compulsive kiss. "So never say 'but' again."

"Even if I say that no word remains after what you said 'but' yes?"

"You can say anything, as long as it ends in yes."

And for the rest of the night, she said almost nothing but yes. She whimpered, whispered and screamed it. She said yes to him, to them, and to everything their future together would bring.

* * *

"You have to tell us, Lili."

Lili turned to the redhead who regarded her with such warm curiosity. Scarlett Kuroshiro, the wife of Raiden, one of Antonio's brothers, was unearthly beautiful. Her husband, who sat beside her, clearly as besotted with her as she appeared to be with him, was Japanese by birth and as gorgeous as she was in his own way. But what truly amazed Lili was their year-old baby daughter, who mixed them both into an incredible mixture. Their adopted children, five of them from four to eight years old, were all playing on the grounds of Antonio's mansion with the other brothers' kids and their nannies.

"Yes, you have to." That was Jenan, another brother's wife, the guy who looked like a genie. Sheikh Numair Al Aswad, the brotherhood's leader. Jenan looked like she'd walked out of *Arabian Nights* herself, and actually *was* a princess. "We must know what you did to Antonio," she said. "What superpowers do you have?"

Lili smirked. "This coming from the pantheon of gods and goddesses Antonio has for brothers and sisters."

Everyone laughed. They'd been laughing every time she'd said anything. It was either that Antonio had given them strict orders to be super delighted with her every word, or that her brand of humor tickled them as much as it did him.

"It's fate." Rafael, the youngest brother, a Brazilian and another juggernaut, hugged his wife, Eliana, into his side tighter. "So our brotherhood would be blessed by the duet of Eliana and Liliana."

Eliana looked adoringly up at her husband before she winked at Lili. "I somehow don't think fate conspired such a perfect match just so your brotherhood would have wives with rhyming names. Besides, I'm Ellie and she's Lili."

"No."

"No."

Both Antonio and Rafael spoke in unison, each vehemently refusing his mate's nickname.

Eliana sighed, giving Lili a we're-in-this-together look. "You're Liliana and never Lili to Antonio, right?"

Lili wiggled one eyebrow at Antonio. "Yeah, and he has exclusive rights to it. So y'all better call me Lili if you want to remain on your doctor's good side."

"It's clear to *me* why Antonio is falling over himself to marry you." That was Richard Graves. Not Antonio's brother, but his partner, the one who smothered them all in security measures, who used to be Rafael's handler. The Brit was the perfect combination of suave and grit, a Bond/Lancelot hybrid. His hand laced with Isabella's, his wife and a surgeon herself, his body touching hers from shoulder to calf, as if he couldn't be away from her. It was weird, since the guy looked as cold as a cobra. "You're a combination I didn't think existed, but exactly what would bowl him over. You must have mowed him down without even trying."

"That she did." Antonio laughed, looking down at her adoringly. "I'm down for the count. For life."

"That's what you guys do. Even those who resist their fate for years." Isabella pinched Richard, who growled and buried a kiss in her neck. She giggled, looking at Lili. "When they give in and give you their hearts, it's yours forever. They'd conquer the world for you, live and die for you. They're a bit scary, but each of them is one-of-a-kind and we can't think how we lived before them."

Richard squeezed his wife tighter as the other women fervently corroborated her statements and their husbands hugged them closer, too.

Lili looked up at Antonio, as usual finding his heart in his eyes, the heart he said he'd grown to love her with.

Pulling him down, she murmured against his lips, "I have no idea at all how."

She surfaced from his drowning kiss to the hoots and claps of the couples, and the disgusted groans of Jakob Wolff, the guy who looked like a Viking marauder, and the only single brother around.

Antonio had just told them about his proposal last night. The ladies had insisted on meeting her at once, and the men had made their wishes come true without delay. They'd all converged on LA from wherever they'd been in the world, arriving at Antonio's mansion one after the other. By the time they'd started arriving, Antonio had told her everything about their previous and current personas, and she'd memorized all the info.

The only one who was missing was Ivan Konstantinov, Antonio's best friend. But he certainly wouldn't have left the side of the woman Antonio had saved that first night she and Antonio were together. Antonio had told her they were missing another brother, but that she wouldn't be seeing him. He'd left their brotherhood six years ago, vowing never to return. It seemed it had been an unspeakable falling-out, since Antonio, who'd so far shared the most horrendous stuff with her, wouldn't say a word about why "Cypher" had left them.

Antonio had wanted their wedding to be three days from now, a whopping week after he'd proposed. But she'd convinced him it was either forgo a wedding completely, or if he wanted an actual party, they needed at least a month. Adamant that there was no way he wasn't giving her a wedding, and reluctant about what he called an unbearable delay, he'd succumbed and set the date.

The evening proceeded in escalating mirth and harmony. Those juggernauts—who between them could rule the world and did to a great degree—and their gorgeous mates promised to be available at all times to help with the wedding preparations. Lili was so delighted with them all, his "family", she kept thanking him for rounding them up for this impromptu engagement party, and thanking them for coming and for being this fantastic.

Everything was so amazing it made her feel she'd plunged into another level of the fairy tale she'd been living with Antonio since that day he'd changed her life. And every now and then one incredulous question floated in her mind.

Could anything in this world be that perfect?

Nine

"My father called again yesterday."

The razor in Antonio's hand stilled over his left cheek. The eyes that had been promising her another session of devastation in the mirror, clean-shaven this time, emptied.

Next second he refocused on shaving, grunting something vague.

Her heart slumped a notch in her chest.

His reaction to the subject of her father and her family was the only thing that marred the perfection they'd been sharing so far.

Her father had been after her to set a date for that reception the Accardis wanted to hold in her honor. When he heard of her engagement, and to whom, his cajoling had become persistence. He couldn't wait to meet her fiancé.

And she couldn't wait for Antonio to meet him, too. Now that she'd been included in Antonio's family, her reluctance to establish a relationship with her father and the Accardis had evaporated. She now wanted to attend the party in which she would meet her long-lost family.

But though Antonio was always eager to do everything with her or for her, joining her for that party wasn't a foregone conclusion. As he'd just proven again.

She tried again. "He's really eager to meet you, and he's hoping I can give him a final answer about the Accardi reception."

Next moment, her heart lodged in her throat. At the shocking burst of wrath and revulsion she saw reflected at her in his eyes.

He suppressed his reaction at once. But she'd seen it.

This was far worse than she'd first thought. It was like this lethal persona that lived within him had surged to the surface. And it had been positively murderous.

Feeling close to tears for thoughtlessly causing him this flare-up, she squeezed her eyes shut and turned to leave the bathroom. "Please, forget it. I shouldn't have brought this up."

"No." She heard the razor clatter in the marble sink, and then the sound of his hurried, powerful footsteps a second before his hands clamped her shoulders and turned her to him. "*Dio mio, mi amore*, no. You should always tell me everything. Everything you want to do, anything on your mind. Always. I beg your forgiveness if I made you feel you can't talk to me about this."

A tear trickled down her cheek, inciting a vicious string of self-abusing expletives from him.

Furious with herself, she wiped it away, pointed at the moisture. "This is for *you*. I hate that I didn't take a hint, cornered you into letting your anger surface. I know how you hate your harsh side, what it takes to curb it so perfectly, to maintain your inner peace. I hate that it's only on my account that you can fall prey again to such aggressive emotions."

Clad in only low-riding black silk pajama bottoms, he scooped her up in his arms, his erection lodging in her quivering belly. "Well, you'll have to live with the fact that I would give up all the peace in existence for the savage emotions you inspire in me, along with the sublime ones. You'll have to make your peace with the fact that I can happily kill for you, not only die for you."

Melting in his hold as he swept her up and carried her to bed, she wrapped her legs around his waist. "Since I'd rather you live for me, thank you very much, let's forget I brought up my father and my family. You probably think I'm stupid to consider accepting his advances. You must consider they more or less did to me what your family did to you."

He started to speak, then clamped his lips. Because she'd put her finger on the truth and he wasn't about to say she didn't. He always told her the truth.

As he came to half lie over her, she cupped his cheek and reveled in his beauty, this god among men who desired her so completely, who was unbelievably hers. "I understand how your anger toward your family extends to mine, and it's totally justified. I wouldn't have considered being anywhere near my father or any of the Accardis on my own. But he's been trying so hard, I wanted to give him a chance before I decide whether to have him in my life. I didn't want unresolved bitterness lurking anywhere if I could work it out. The best I expected was that my family would be a once-a-year presence in my life, and my father would be a peripheral one.

"But that was before I realized how forcefully you feel about this. *Nothing* is worth making you suffer the least discomfort. You, and our lives together, are the only things that matter to me. I *did* mean it when I said let's just forget about this."

Antonio stared down at his woman, the woman he'd been falling deeper in love with each passing second.

Every time she'd mentioned her father and their joint family, his agitation had built. Though he now considered whatever debt they owed him paid a million times over just for being the reason he'd met Liliana, he abhorred their very existence. He never wanted to see any of them, not to punish them or to have anything to do with them. But the idea that they were trying to enter her life, when they were bound to taint it, made his loathing mount. He'd destroy them all before he let them cause her the least heartache.

But she needed closure and now, because she considered only him and his feelings, she was dismissing that need.

And there was no way he'd deprive her of anything at all. He'd swallow his hatred, hell, he'd swallow molten steel if it provided her with peace. On the off chance that her father and his family brought her a measure of contentment, he'd even tolerate them. He'd be there for her, with her, at every event, honoring her and showing them she had a lethal protector in him. Just in case any of them thought to show their true colors.

He gathered her closer, delighting in her feel, her love. "We'll forget nothing. I'm going to meet your father, and we're going to New York to meet your family." Anxiety flared again in her reddened eyes. He caught her lips in a cherishing kiss, aborting her protest. "We'll do everything that might provide you with even a remote possibility of well-being, always. And that, *mi amore*, is that."

Flying to New York on Antonio's private jet, Lili felt she'd plunged deeper into the parallel universe she'd stumbled into since the day he'd entered her life.

The Accardis had set the reception for the very next weekend, two days after Antonio had insisted they accept their invitation. The haste had to be her father's doing, no doubt. But this meant that the first time Antonio met him would be at the reception.

All the way, Antonio had placated her worries about his aversion to her family. He assured her if she enjoyed knowing them, he'd be lenient and might even consider liking them. After all, she made him so happy he could forgive any past transgressions and afford to be magnanimous like her. That had reassured her, until they entered the Accardi family mansion.

Now she felt something writhing inside him. Something dark and vicious.

Before she told him she would leave if he didn't want to be here after all, her father came rushing toward them as soon as they crossed the mansion's threshold.

In the seconds before he reached them, his smile as wide as humanly possible, Lili noticed something for the first time. Her father and Antonio looked alike. Apart from the size and age difference—Antonio was much bigger, and her father had wrinkles and silver hair—the two men shared the same bone structure and skin tone. If she'd seen them on the streets, she would have thought them relatives. In fact, if someone saw the three of them, with her looking like her mother, people would have thought it was Antonio who was her father's son.

"*Mia bella Lilianissima*, you're here!"

Feeling Antonio going rigid beside her, she stood with a wooden smile, awkwardly letting her father hug her.

Thankfully, he did so more briefly than in the few times she'd seen him. For now he had a distraction in Antonio.

"Dr. Balducci, a hundred welcomes to Casa Accardi."

"One would do, Signore Accardi." Antonio took her father's extended hand after a telling hesitation, as if he loathed touching him. He still managed a courteous nod, for her sake.

Oblivious to Antonio's aversion, her father enfolded Antonio's hand in both of his fervently. "I'm beyond delighted about your and Lili's engagement. Only the best man is worthy of her, and that's what I hear you are. And an Italian, too. It's just perfection. Everything is coming together in the exact perfect way that my incomparable daughter deserves."

As if he'd reached his limit, Antonio withdrew his hand from her father's grip. "Liliana is beyond incomparable, and deserves only the best of everything. Which I'll make sure she gets, now and forever."

Antonio's words sounded like a warning. He was telling her father he'd better be on his best behavior with her, or else.

Her nerves jangled at Antonio's barely veiled threat. Regardless of whether her father deserved it for his past behavior, she'd hoped her fiancé would offer him that leniency he'd talked about. It was clear Antonio wouldn't offer any until her father proved himself. Which she was sure Antonio wouldn't make easy.

Not that her father noticed any subscript in Antonio's words. He now led them to the open doors at the end of the expansive entrance hall, from which the sounds of music and conversation were emanating. "Between us, we're going to make sure of that, Dr. Balducci." Her father looked at him expectantly. "Can I call you Antonio?"

"If you wish." That was said in the tone of "don't you dare." Antonio looked so forbidding it was only thanks to her father's enthusiastic obliviousness that he hadn't turned to stone. Then his voice plunged into the subzero domain. "I understand you had no contact with Liliana as she grew up. Now, in your new eagerness to know her, I keep wondering what could possibly explain the years of absence and silence."

Her father stopped, looking as if Antonio had just handed him the best gift he'd ever had. "I'm *so* glad you asked! I tried to explain to Lili when I contacted her after

Luanne's death. But she always insisted what was past was past."

Yeah. She hadn't wanted to hear his reasons. She could establish some kind of relationship with him not knowing them. But if she knew them and found them pathetic or unacceptable, she wouldn't be able to go forward in any kind of relationship with him.

Her father clamped her and Antonio's arms. "Come, please. This can't be told with dozens of nosy Accardis around."

Her father rushed them to an old-fashioned smoking room filled with burgundy leather chesterfields, Persian rugs and dark wood paneling. Though everything was authentic and antique, it showed the weight of time and clearly hadn't had any recent maintenance. Though the three-hundred-year-old mansion was imposing, it wasn't in the prime condition she'd expected from such an elite family.

After her father sat them down side by side, he stood before them as if to give the performance he'd been waiting for all his life.

Then he began. "Luanne was glorious, very much like you, my beloved Lili, at least in looks and in her brilliant mind. Unorthodox, independent, a trailblazer. I fell in love with her on sight in Saint Mark's Basilica, as I believe she did with me. She told me she was the only child of a single mother who also worked in the medical field, that all she'd known since childhood had been academic endeavor and excellence."

So she'd been living her mother's life. Until Antonio.

"She'd just finished her medical residency and was about to start her fellowship when she discovered she hadn't actually lived yet. So before she plunged into her hospital work she'd decided to take two years to roam the world. Italy was her first stop.

"We spent every minute together for two weeks until she said she was heading north. I was besotted with her, but knew I'd never see her again if she left, so I proposed. She was stunned, refused on the spot, left the next day. So I followed her, all over Europe. My mother and uncles were enraged. I'd just taken my father's place in the family law firm, which I'd trained all my life to do, and I left them in the lurch. Then Luanne finally succumbed and we got married in France, but when we went home, no one was happy. Not only had my desertion caused the firm irredeemable losses, but I was supposed to marry to benefit the family. But I wanted none of that. I told them I wouldn't take my father's place permanently, that I wanted to leave and be with Luanne and the baby we knew by then we'd made. You, my darling girl."

Her throat tightening with every word, she leaned closer into Antonio, who intensified his hold on her as if protecting her from her father's revelations.

Her father went on, his gaze looking backward in time. "My mother told me Luanne wasn't wife material, would make a terrible mother, that I'd destroy my life and yours if I remained with her. Luanne hated my mother, too, hated all the Accardis and their elitism, hated being in Venice, and in what she called a moldy dwelling fit only for monsters and ghosts.

"When our stay in Venice lengthened and Luanne gave birth to you while I took care of the problems my absence caused, she started believing I'd never stand up for myself or for you, that I'd remain under my family's boot forever. To prove that only she and you mattered, I set a date for when I'd leave it all behind and go back with her to the States.

"At first, she was ecstatic. But as your first birthday neared and I was getting ready to leave, she began asking me what I would do there while she worked. Stay home and raise you? I knew nothing but the law, but I wouldn't be able to continue that in the States. My family threatened to disown me if I left them again, which would have left me penniless, but I didn't care. Then on your first birthday, Luanne told me she no longer wanted me, that I was suffocating her, that she wanted me and my family out of her life. Out of yours, too.

"I was convinced she was suffering from prolonged and severe postpartum depression. I told her so and she broke down. She wept and wept and begged me to let her go. My heart broke, but I couldn't reach her. I could only say that whatever happened between us, I would remain your father. I had rights to you, and you had a right to me. Her misery deepened as she asked how I would be your father across continents. What would it do to you, always waiting for a father who'd come only when my family let me go? How many times a year would that be and for how long? I insisted I'd manage something regular, but she thought it would only keep her and you in purgatory forever.

"After I failed to soothe her and her health declined, I was forced to grant her a divorce, but I gave her all the money I had. I wanted her to buy a beautiful house in an upscale neighborhood, to have enough money to bring you up in luxury, so she never had to work too hard and could be with you more. Problem was, only a portion of the money was mine. The rest was family funds. I thought I'd manage paying it back before anyone found out, but they did.

"They went after her for the money and things escalated. I was helpless to stop it from spiraling into an ugly legal fight. During the proceedings, my family even tried to get custody of you, claiming she was unbalanced. That was when she told me she never wanted to see me again, that she'd already told you I didn't want to see you, and that my family were horrible people who wanted to throw you out on the streets. I still came regularly through the years, trying to see you, but she wouldn't let me. She said you were stable and hardworking and the last thing you needed was the upheaval of my erratic presence and the influence of my evil family.

"By the time you became an adult and I could approach you without her consent, you'd had too many years without knowing me. I knew she'd turn it into a fight over you, causing you the upheaval she said she protected you from. I felt I already failed you, so... I gave up.

"When she became ill, I installed a lump sum in a new account in her name, asked her attorney and bank to let you think it was a backup plan she always had, and gave you full control of it, so her care didn't burden you, at least financially. *Dio mio, figlia mia,* my daughter, I wanted to be there for you, but I didn't know what to say. I didn't want to blame her for anything in her condition. But the moment I heard of her death, I had to try again. She wasn't there to be hurt if your opinion of her changed, or for you to be torn between us. And...here we are."

It all added up. Knowing her mother, Lili accepted this as a plausible explanation. It shed a new, understandable light on the Accardis and a favorable one on her father.

Before she could get any words past the vise gripping her throat, her father bent over her, taking her hands in his. "I don't ask that you forgive me for not fighting harder to be your father. I only hope you'll give me the chance to be in your life now, in any way. Like your future groom, I believe you deserve only the best, and I hope you'll give me the privilege of doing my best to provide you with it."

And she found herself in his arms, hugging him and being hugged by him, the father she'd never had, but would now have for as long as life allowed them.

After her father deluged her in apologies, and obtained

her promise to let him into her life, she turned to Antonio. He was on his feet, muscles bunched, gaze pinned on them.

Unable to read his expression, she reached out to him.

He at once claimed her to his side, wincing down at her. "*Mi amore,* your tears kill me, even ones of happiness."

Blubbering a laugh, she wrapped her arms around him. "You'll have to withstand those. It's not every day that I get my father back." She met his turbulent gaze and smiled, asking him silently for his blessing.

As he took her trembling lips, he murmured against them for her ears only. "He can call me Antonio."

Whooping with delight, she invited her father closer, hugging him with her other arm. "You can call him Antonio."

Realizing the significance of that, her father poured jubilation all over them. After getting confirmations that they'd make use of him in their wedding preparations, and anything else, for life, he led them back to where the Accardis awaited them en masse.

Entering the ballroom tucked into Antonio's protection, Lili boggled at the number of polished elites who queued to introduce themselves.

Not that she thought their regard had anything to do with her. They were here at her father's demand, to make a grand gesture in his atonement campaign. But all the awe everyone exhibited was on Antonio's behalf.

The night blurred from then on. The only thing she registered clearly was Antonio's simmering intensity. He might have sanctioned her father's story and had acquitted him of being a cold-blooded deserter, but it was clear the Accardis hadn't passed his test.

Then suddenly, the unease she felt in Antonio spiked to something else. Something darker.

Trying to understand why, she paid extra attention to

the people who'd just come forward, but she found nothing different about them.

Before she could probe the situation further, her father pulled her away while Antonio remained held back by the newcomers.

As she greeted two more of her father's cousins twice removed, her focus remained on Antonio as he frowned at those who thronged around him. Then one of the two men said something to her that made her give him her full attention.

"You'll go down in the annals of our family history as the one who saved us all, Lili." At her incomprehension, he elaborated, "As you may know, our family businesses are intertwined, and over a year ago, some bad stock market decisions led to a domino effect in all our holdings. Dr. Balducci, through his Black Castle division, offered to bail us out, saving us from the impasse—that has since regretfully worsened—in return for acquiring our major ancestral assets."

The other man nodded. "We two were the ones charged with conveying the family's decision to turn down his offer. The damned family rules dictate those assets stay within the family at any cost. I can't tell you how relieved everyone is now that we can finally accept his offer, since he *will* be family shortly."

"*If* his offer is still on the table," said the other man.

The first man winked at her. "If it isn't, we're sure you, dear Lili, can convince him to put it back there."

As her father exclaimed that he'd never heard of this, Lili's gaze sought out Antonio again, her mind spinning.

He'd never mentioned it. So maybe he hadn't been involved and it had been his brokers trolling for acquisitions?

No, there was no way he wouldn't be in charge of every offer issuing from his organization. So why hadn't he told her about this aborted transaction involving her family?

Could it have slipped his mind? That was again something she found impossible to believe. Nothing slipped
Antonio's mind.

Could part of his tension around her family be on account of the thwarted deal? And it continued in part because he didn't know yet that it would go through? Did he
know their engagement would provide a solution to this
deadlock?

Whoa. It seemed she could still slide back into insecurity. She thought she'd stopped wondering why Antonio
wanted to marry her, stopped looking for reasons besides
that he loved her.

But this deal certainly couldn't be even a contributing
reason. The financial benefit would all be her family's in
their current bind. At best, the acquisitions could have
only minor value to him compared with his other assets.

Dismissing her absurd thoughts, she concluded her side
meeting, laughingly promising the two men to put in a
good word for them with Antonio.

As she rejoined him, his mind seemed to be elsewhere
as he received her, his gaze leaving her whenever anyone
came to talk to them to fix on one certain part of the ballroom. She followed it and saw the same relatives who'd
first made him tense up.

By the time he asked her if she didn't mind leaving,
she'd had enough tension for one night and eagerly agreed.

Her unease lingered until the moment they entered their
hotel suite. Then he swept her up in his arms, threw her
down on the bed and took her with an even more ferocious
hunger than ever before. Flesh on flesh, he melted her dis-
quiet and bound her deeper under his spell.

In the next week, her family members competed to invite them to their homes.

Antonio gave her carte blanche to accept all invitations,

though it meant flying all over the country. His brother-hood family had taken up the slack in the arrangements for their wedding and kept them apprised of all developments, so they could afford the time to get to know hers better.

As the visits started, a new discomfort crept over her. Though he seemed willing to know everyone for her sake, and she was grateful since there were some members she liked and wished to know better, she soon noticed his focus was on one woman. One of those he'd tensed around dur-ing the reception. She'd become a common denominator in all the gatherings.

Sofia Accardi.

Sofia, her father's third cousin, was in her late fifties, but looked like a great mid-forties. She oozed charisma and distinction and she seemed intensely interested in Anto-nio. Her children—her daughters especially—were pres-ent on most occasions, flocking around him like moths to the flame.

Then Sofia invited them to her home, despite it being in the midst of a major renovation. When Lili said they'd come later when the work was done, the woman was in-sistent. It was Antonio who ended the debate, accepting the invitation.

It was insidious—the feeling Lili had that Antonio had consented to every invitation so far only so it wouldn't look strange when they accepted Sofia's. The woman he'd re-mained stilted around all week.

Now as the day progressed at Sofia's estate, everything Lili felt from Antonio intensified her suspicions.

Sofia *did* provoke something inside him. Something vol-canic in intensity. Could it be...attraction? Lust? Worse?

Sofia, though older, was incredibly beautiful and vo-luptuous, a very sensual woman who was known as a man-eater, having gone through three husbands and un-counted lovers. Lili, in her relative inexperience, felt decidedly lacking compared to the woman who was more on his level than she would ever be.

After dinner, while she was trapped in conversation with Sofia's daughters, Antonio, who'd said almost nothing to her all evening, walked out of the family room. And her agitation boiled over.

She couldn't wait until they left. She had to find him, ask him, now. If he was having second thoughts of any sort, this was the time to come clean.

As she excused herself, she realized it wasn't only Antonio who was unaccounted for. Sofia, too, had disappeared.

Feeling like her whole world was sinking under her feet, she went in search of them through the immense house.

The areas under renovation were barricaded, so that left only the private quarters. The bedrooms. Nowhere a guest like Antonio would be. It couldn't…he *wouldn't*…

Suddenly she heard his voice. An emotion-filled growl.

It was followed by a husky, pleading moan. Sofia's.

Her heart almost uprooted itself in her chest and every muscle trembled as she stepped through a door she hadn't noticed was ajar in the dimness of the corridor, one a barricade announced off-limits.

The room inside was pitch-dark, but its French windows opened to a terrace, from which their voices emanated.

Then she saw them.

In the lights coming from the garden, under the canopy of a starlit night, Antonio stood like a monolith with his back almost to her as Sofia hugged him frantically.

Then slowly, as if he couldn't resist anymore, his arms wrapped around her.

Ten

Lili froze.

The sight in front of her... Antonio, with another woman...

There was nothing. No more air. No more heartbeats.

Then the woman's lament pierced her like a bullet. "You have to believe me, Antonio. I never wanted to give you up."

The agony the words contained lodged like an ax in her chest.

They...they had a previous affair? And Antonio still felt that fiercely for her? Still loved her? But he'd said *she* was his first love. He'd said he'd grown a heart to love *her*.

Antonio pushed Sofia away on a butchered groan, as if tearing himself from her arms hurt him, badly. The sound of his torment made Lili shrivel.

Had he been with her only because he'd thought Sofia had abandoned him? Because he couldn't have her? And now that he evidently could, he was fighting his desire for her?

But Lili didn't want him honor-bound or obligated. If he didn't love and desire her as completely as she did him, she only wished him to have what he wanted. If that was no longer her, she had to set him free. Now. *Now.*

Before she could force her numb legs to move, Sofia started sobbing, and what she said robbed Lili of all power, made her sag to her knees.

"I held you only once after my C-section when I was still drowsy from anesthesia. You were the most perfect baby boy."

Sofia was…was…*his mother.*

"When I fully came to, my family had sent you away. I threatened to kill myself if they didn't return you but they told me it was too late, that an undisclosed adopter took you. I went mad. I tried to commit suicide." She extended her hands to him so he could see the scars she still bore. "After I was saved, I knew I'd been stupid, since I couldn't find you if I died. But there seemed no way to find anything about you, and I fell into a deep depression. Three years later I met my first husband, and he promised to help me find you. But his investigations only discovered that my parents and uncle had lied, that they'd put you in an orphanage. When Mark found out which one, I eloped with him and we went to the orphanage. But you were no longer there and we couldn't find your trail. I drove myself insane imagining you'd fallen into the worst of hands."

A vicious huff crackled from Antonio. "You can't even imagine the kind of hands I fell into. They make slave traders look like Good Samaritans."

The sob that tore through Sofia sounded as if it had ripped her apart inside. She reached her hands out to him.

"Don't." He pulled away, as if her touch would burn him. "I don't need your pity or your guilt. As you can see, I far more than survived."

She tried to approach again before her hands fell to her sides, defeated. "You're right. I can't even imagine what you went through, or how you conquered your horrific beginnings and then the world. I can only tell you my side, how I lived with the trauma of your loss, of imagining your fate." A sob choked her, soaked her voice in tears. "But I did always feel you were out there, alive, strong. Then I saw a photo of you in a magazine and felt that I knew you. Then I saw you face-to-face and felt the connection between us. Your half siblings felt it, too, even if they couldn't imagine what drew them to you like that. I thought I was crazy, but the way you looked at me, at them, made me hope you felt it, too. But today, I just *knew* who you are, and that you know who I am. I felt you didn't want me to acknowledge our relationship. But I had to do it. Had to tell you I recognized you, that losing you tore a hole in my soul that nothing has ever mended, not even having more children, or adopting two boys who reminded me of you. My father and uncle died years ago, and my mother is now senile, but I still curse them every day as I did for the past forty years, for what they did to you and to me."

This time, when she reached for him, he let her cling to his arms. She looked up at him, her eyes beseeching. "I know I can never undo what's been done to you. I can't do *anything...*" Another harsh sob escaped her throat. "Nothing but hope that you'll let me know you, and maybe one day, in some way, I'll make it up to you."

Lili was a mess of tremors. Sofia's impassioned confession shook her far more than her father's had. To imagine what some of those Accardis—his family like they were hers—had cost him, was beyond endurance.

Then he finally spoke, his voice darker than the night. "When I discovered what your family did to me, what I thought you agreed to, I planned to exact punishment, on you and on the whole family whose rules dictate throwing away unwanted children. I wanted to buy your ancestral assets, lure you all into a merger with the promise of saving you from bankruptcy, so I'd end up in control of your very lives, before I took my time destroying you, each in the way you deserve. But even in their desperation, the Accardis rejected my life raft because, of all the irony, I wasn't 'family'."

The realization hit Lili so hard she felt her head would burst with it. What she'd always felt but couldn't even guess at. The reason he'd approached her in the first place.

He'd needed an in into the family.

It had been her.

That was why he'd pursued her, why he'd proposed to her.

It all made sense now. He'd never loved her. Never even wanted her. He'd only wanted revenge. She'd been nothing but his means to his lifelong retribution.

The blow of realization was so brutal it interrupted her very heartbeats.

"But now after you told me how—"

Antonio's words were suddenly cut off as he tensed and turned to look in Lili's direction.

There was no way he could see her in the darkness. And she hadn't made a sound. She couldn't move, couldn't even breathe.

"Liliana?"

He did feel her. Or it was her devastation he felt. Now she realized that everything between them had been a lie.

Suffocating, feeling she'd rather die than face him now, she scrambled up, stumbling as she ran back out of the room.

"Liliana!"

His shout punched her between the shoulder blades, intensifying her desperation.

She had to escape him, escape the agony. But she couldn't pass through the others on her way out. She had to find another exit.

Spilling into the next barricaded room, which must open onto the same wraparound veranda leading to the garden, she rushed to open the closed French doors, growing frantic as his thundering footsteps drew closer, his shout begging her to stop another lash propelling her forward, making her more frantic.

Then everything happened at once. Sofia's shrill warning, Antonio roaring, and she was falling.

Pain exploded, sharp and searing, tearing through her midriff. A simultaneous agony splintered through her thigh, almost fracturing her awareness.

Then she was on her back, staring up at the stars as they blurred, the night darkening around her.

The whoosh of blood in her ears receded, only to be replaced by Antonio's frenzy as he begged her not to move.

Not that she could. Even drawing enough oxygen not to pass out was excruciating. She lay there, paralyzed with pain, watching his massive silhouette, an avenging angel jumping down a steep drop to crouch over her.

Vaguely, she realized the veranda she'd tried to escape through wasn't there. She'd fallen through its skeleton, getting stabbed on the way down by protruding concrete-reinforcing steel bars. From the agony now emanating from her left side, she realized she must have damaged some internal organs. Probably her spleen, intestines, maybe a kidney. Her left femur was also fractured. Muscle damage was a given, maybe nerve damage, too.

She couldn't see Antonio's face, could only hear his strident breathing as he swept her in the bright beam of a flashlight.

Then she heard the tremor of dread in his voice as he pressed down on her side. He'd assessed her injuries and was applying pressure to slow the bleeding. "I'm here, *mi amore*, I've got you. Just don't move."

"*Dio mio, dio mio*, is she…?"

Without looking up, he hissed, "Leave *now*, Sofia. Tell no one."

Sofia's gasp at Antonio's harshness carried to Lili's wavering consciousness, but the woman complied, disappearing from Lili's field of vision. Then Antonio started talking, barking sharp, concise orders. To Paolo, to fetch his medical kit from the limo. To his pilot, to get a helicopter. To the medical center, to prepare his OR.

Working at top efficiency, Antonio, the miracle worker who put people back together, had everything ready in minutes to reconstruct her. After he'd broken her, torn her apart.

He bent over her, raining frantic kisses all over her face. "You're going to be okay, *mi amore*, I promise."

She tried to cringe away. "You…shouldn't…"

"Don't talk. Just let me take care of you."

"You shouldn't…" Her teeth clattered, more with desolation than with blood loss or pain. "…have done…this to me…"

A groan escaped him, his shudder transmitting to her trembling body. "Whatever you heard, whatever you understood, whatever you think I did, you're wrong, *mi amore*, I swear."

Tears oozed out of her very soul. "I…loved…you…"

"And I worship you. You're everything to me. *Everything*."

All light faded, taking his image with it as blackness sucked her under. "I—I think…it's better…this way…"

As she slipped away, she wished it would be forever. So

she wouldn't live knowing she'd never had him, or with the agony that would never go away.

Antonio watched Liliana's eyes flutter closed, felt her bloodied body going limp and still, and went mad.

His roar almost tore out the heart that had been exploding with every beat since he'd watched her plunge into that jagged maw of concrete and steel.

He'd done this to her. This was his fault. All of it.

She was lying here, torn and broken, because he'd lied to her. Because he'd overridden her disinclination and accepted his mother's invitation. Because she must have picked up on his weirdness, because he'd left her behind without explanation, making her follow him, hear what had made her escape him so desperately through the house they shouldn't have been in.

If he lost her…

No. He'd *never* lose her. He *would* save her. He'd pay his very life and far more to restore her, body and heart.

But before he could do anything, he had to suppress the insanity of terror and the violence of self-hatred. He had to go through his perfected motions. Everything he'd ever learned, every skill he'd acquired, every bit of experience he'd accumulated through the long years of slavery and struggle and success, had all been for this moment.

Everything he was had been made for her. Everything he could do, he'd learned to save her.

From the injuries he'd caused her.

Antonio raced against time in a crazed fast-forward, spiraling through all levels of hell.

In what seemed like minutes, he'd flown Liliana to his nearest medical center where he'd had to cut her open, literally this time, so he could mend her. He'd poured all his expertise, all his being, into saving her. It had driven him insane, not only the extent of her injuries and the reason she'd sustained them, but the feeling that she was resisting his efforts. He might have been unhinged with terror and guilt, but he did feel as if she wanted him to fail.

It had been when she'd flatlined, when there'd been no medical reason anymore that she should, that he'd become sure.

She'd wanted to die.

In the horrific lifetime until he'd managed to restart her heart, he'd known. If he'd failed, his heart would have stopped seconds after hers.

Now she lay in the ICU, just like Ivan's mystery woman had three weeks ago. But the latter had fought to survive. He could feel Liliana still fighting to escape. He'd hurt her so much, it was as if she didn't want to wake up to face the agony.

Some of her last words revolved in his mind again, hacking it to pieces. *You shouldn't have done this to me. I loved you.*

He'd been a coward, avoiding a confession that could have caused a passing crisis, a pain he could have healed. He'd been self-deluding, thinking she wouldn't pick up on the turmoil that racked him every time he saw his mother. Liliana had always felt he'd been hiding something, but because of his evasions, when she'd overheard him, she'd concluded the worst. What had once been the truth.

And it had destroyed her.

Sagging to his knees beside her bed, he let the tears he'd never shed before pour out of his very soul.

"You're my life, *mi amore*. I can't and won't live without you. I beg you, don't punish me by harming yourself."

In response, her vitals only grew more erratic.

Exploding to his feet, he rummaged for medications, roaring for his assistants to prepare emergency resuscitation.

Just as he was about to inject the cocktail into her drip, a deep voice broke over him.

"I don't think she needs that."

He swung around to blast whoever was interfering, then rocked on his feet with the aborted aggression when he saw Ivan.

His head nurse was scurrying away. Had she fetched Ivan to deal with him? He sure would have blasted her, as he'd done every member of his medical team all night.

Ivan approached him as if he were approaching a wounded tiger. "I know she doesn't need that because you never second-guess yourself, never up your meds. You get it right the first time. Always."

"But it's *Liliana*. And I doubt I'm even sane anymore."

Ivan's hand clamped his, forced it down. "Come with me, Tonio."

He glared at his friend through his tears. "She needs—"

"She needs you to leave her alone for now." Ivan dragged him away, his pull inexorable in Antonio's shaken state. "You told me…*she* would feel me in her sleep, and it would give her strength, make her fight. When she woke up, she told me it was true. Now your lady feels you, too, and to me it looks like your presence distresses her. You might be the very thing compromising her survival."

It killed Antonio to admit this had to be the explanation. There was no medical reason why Liliana shouldn't be stable.

Letting Ivan tug him to the observation area, he sagged down, his gaze pinned on Liliana's inert figure and inanimate face. He plummeted into a deeper hell of guilt and desperation.

It was only when Ivan's assessment proved right and Liliana's vitals stabilized that he finally choked out, "How did you know? How did you come?"

"Paolo called me, and I called the others. As for how…

she insisted she is stable, can spare me for hours and told me to go to you. If it had been a choice between being by her side or yours…"

"You would have chosen her." Antonio looked back at Liliana. "I'd choose her, too, over anything or anyone. Starting with myself."

Just then, his brothers and their mates began arriving.

It wasn't long before he told them to go away. His sanity was hanging by a thread, and their empathy, their every bolstering word, the very sight of them together, was about to snap it.

Finally, they reluctantly left, with Ivan promising he'd keep them updated. He told Ivan his presence wasn't helping anymore, to leave, too, but the icy Russian just ignored him.

As the last of his brothers disappeared from view, Ivan turned to him. "I take it from your condition, and her unconscious reaction to your presence, this isn't just an accident?"

Suddenly feeling the crushing need to share everything with his oldest and closest friend, Antonio told Ivan everything.

After he fell silent, Ivan's gaze grew contemplative. "This is good for you, you know?" Anger exploded inside Antonio, making him lunge to grab Ivan by the lapels. Ivan crushed his hands in the vise of his, forcing him to listen. "You were always too serene, too untouchable. I always knew this meant what's inside you was even more nightmarish than any of us. And this woman has reached inside you and dragged out your chaos, so she could dispel it. She also released every emotion you never thought yourself capable of."

"She created them. And I am the reason she's lying there. Because I lied to her, because she thinks I never loved her."

Ivan shrugged. "But you'll prove you do, and that you had some stupidly noble reason for hiding what you hid from her. But even if she thinks you don't love her now, I suspect deep down she feels that you do, since she's found the perfect method to brutally punish you."

"I'd take any punishment but this." His eyes burned with more tears.

"But this is what she's choosing, even unconsciously, hurting you by showing you how you hurt her. So you'll take it, until she believes you've had enough, until *you* believe you've atoned. Then if everything the brothers say about her and what she feels for you is true, she'll take you back."

Antonio didn't even dare hope it would be that easy, or that it would come to pass at all. But somehow Ivan's prophecy stopped the spiral of madness. He couldn't have Liliana wake up to find him totally deranged.

And she *would* wake up. He'd transplant his very life into her if that was what it took. He would have her whole again at any price.

For the next two days as Liliana remained asleep, Antonio discovered that hell was bottomless.

He'd forced himself to heed Ivan's theory that her deterioration was directly proportionate to his proximity. Though despondent, he'd watched her from afar, every second he could.

On the third day she woke up while one of his assistants was tending her. He watched every nuance of her return to consciousness, then awareness, feeling as if he were waiting for a verdict of life or death.

Her lashes fluttered open, a hand jerking when she found herself hooked up to drips and monitors. Her whole body tensed before slumping back, realization replacing confusion on her face.

Through the open mike where he'd listened to her every breath, he heard his nurse explaining her condition and reassuring her. Liliana only listened, but as his assistant finished checking her, she said something he couldn't hear in her ear.

A minute later his assistant came out and, with a wide smile, told him he'd pulled off another miracle. Liliana was far better than expected after such an extensive surgery.

And she'd asked to see him.

Afraid to breathe, to hope, he didn't know when he'd moved, but he found himself standing over Liliana.

She spoke without raising her eyes, her voice hoarse from intubation, chafing his every nerve ending. "Thank you for saving my life. Even if you no longer need me."

He must have misheard her. She couldn't have said… "What?"

Her eyes rose to him now, but they were no longer hers, but a stranger's. "Since you've revealed yourself to your mother, I'm sure you can now enter my—your family to destroy it from within on your own."

He didn't know how he remained standing. He'd thought there could be no more pain than what he'd suffered in the past three days. He'd known nothing.

This, what she believed, was true agony.

"*Per Dio*, am I that big a monster in your eyes now?"

"You're a vigilante, and you do what needs to be done to achieve your goal no matter the price. You're also a surgeon and you save patients regardless of their value to you."

"You think I considered you just another patient?" he choked out, unable to believe how horrible it had all become.

"It's a fact you no longer need me."

"I will need you, and only you, till my dying breath."

Her gaze emptied more. "You probably didn't wish it

to end this way. I do realize you must feel bad about my injuries—"

He cut across her mutilating words. "I don't feel bad, Liliana, I feel devastated."

"You shouldn't. I'm responsible for what happened to me. I barged into clearly labeled danger zones, repeatedly."

Both the under-construction site, and his life.

He gritted his teeth against the mounting pain. "What devastates me is that I destroyed your faith in me, in yourself, so completely. And it's why you almost...almost..."

"But I didn't die, thanks to you." She surveyed his agitation with a blank look, as lifeless as her voice. "And I do understand your need for exacting retribution on the family that threw you away. If only you'd told me in the beginning, I'd have helped you, if only for the possibility you'd find a peaceful and just resolution, and you wouldn't have needed to go to these lengths to use me as your stealth weapon."

"You must believe me, *mi amore*. Whatever I intended to do, I abandoned it all after I first saw you. I wanted only you since."

As if she hadn't heard him, she went on, "But now that you discovered you've misjudged your mother even worse than I have my father, I hope you'll reconsider your revenge. The guilty ones are either dead or as good as. And I doubt no one else, no matter their faults, deserves your wrath. I hope you won't destroy everyone indiscriminately for the crimes of some of their own. And that you'll give your mother the chance she hoped for."

It agonized him more that even in her own devastation she was thinking of others.

He dropped to his knees beside her, his hand trembling as he took hers. "I avoided even talking about your family, not only because none of them mattered anymore, but because I was afraid they'd hurt you. I only agreed to meet them when I realized how much you needed to settle their issue, and to be there to protect you from them. It turned out the only one I needed to protect you from was myself. And I failed. I failed you."

"I failed myself. And now I'll have the scars to remind me never to do so again."

Before he took her hand to his lips, she pulled it away with surprising strength, as if she could no longer bear his touch. She turned her head away, closing her eyes. Her dry eyes.

It was as if she had nothing left to say to him. As if she had nothing left inside her.

He remained on his knees beside her as depletion claimed her again, at last learning the meaning of helplessness.

During the next two weeks, as Liliana recuperated, Antonio never left the center, always hovering around, trying again and again to get her to talk to him. But after that time when she'd first woken up, she'd given him nothing but silence. His presence seemed to plunge her into deepening despondency.

Everyone kept telling him to let her bounce back from the trauma, that she was hurt that much because she loved him as fiercely and that he'd eventually heal her with his love. But the days had passed and Liliana seemed to be drawing further into herself.

And today he couldn't bear it anymore. He'd just entered her room, said he would stand there beside her bed, no matter how long it took, until she talked to him again.

Then she finally did, and shattered his heart.

Eyes no longer distant, raw, ravished, she looked up at him, her pain and betrayal skewering him to his vitals. "You lied to me, Antonio, when all I ever asked of you was honesty. Even if you've developed feelings for me, everything that you said or did, everything that happened between us, is tainted by this lie. Now I can't trust or feel again. My emotions, my faith, like the body you've put back together, have been damaged and will remain scarred."

Before he could swear to her that he'd wait forever for her to heal, that he'd erase her scars, she sat up, swung her good leg followed by her casted leg over the side of the bed. "There's no more medical reason for me to remain here. I want you to discharge me."

All he wanted to do was rave and rant and keep her there until she gave him another chance.

But he couldn't press her more in her fragile state.

"I will. But please, Liliana, whatever you think of me or however you feel now, *please*, come back with me to our place, let me take care of you as you recuperate."

She shook her head, and for the first time since her accident tears started to fall. He hated himself more with every track of moisture that stained her pale cheeks.

He wished *she'd* rave and rant. Her subdued misery was so much worse than any passionate display that would have given him hope he could revive her emotions.

All he could do now was stop hurting her more, let her go and hope she'd heal enough one day to let him in again. Pray that she wouldn't shut him out like her mother had her father, for the rest of her life.

The day that should have been their wedding day came and went in total silence from Liliana.

She hadn't gone back to Antonio's mansion. And she hadn't returned to the lab.

He was hailed as the leading expert of mending catastrophic injuries, but he'd injured the one person he needed to live, an injury he was helpless to heal.

It was during one of the surgeries he now buried himself in that he realized the truth.

It didn't matter that he healed her so she'd come back to him. It mattered that she healed for herself, so she could resume her life, her work. He and what he felt were of no consequence.

Only she mattered.

And because only she did, if her emotional health depended on letting her go, he would.

Even if it destroyed him.

Eleven

Three months after the accident, though Lili had fully recovered physically, she hadn't gone back to work.

Among those who regularly came visiting, Brian had been the one who kept persistently trying to convince her to do so. She'd insisted right back that she'd decided to take all her missed vacations at once.

Ever since Antonio had discharged her and sent her back to LA on his private jet, she'd left the house only for follow-ups and the intensive physiotherapy Antonio had scheduled for her, both performed by others under his command.

She hadn't seen or heard from him since.

At times, longing for him made her unable to breathe.

Her father, whom she'd told a severely edited version of the truth, had been adamant it meant she'd healed enough to believe in Antonio's love again. But she knew missing him had nothing to do with being over the trauma. Missing him, with every breath, had always been her default.

As for his love, after being dedicated to her after the accident, he had been silent since he'd discharged her. Whatever he'd felt for her, it seemed she'd pushed him away so hard he'd given up on her.

She couldn't heed her father's fervent advice to contact him. She couldn't impose on him if he'd moved on.

She was indulging in what had become an obsession, driving herself insane again wondering if he'd ever really loved her and if she'd killed his love, or if he'd discovered he didn't feel enough for her after all, when her doorbell rang.

Since everyone called before passing by, the hope that it was Antonio propelled her to the door the fastest she'd moved since the accident.

But it wasn't him on her doorstep. It was Sofia Accardi.

After exchanging a long stare, Lili stunned and disappointed, Sofia discomfited and tentative, Lili invited her in. Questions flooded her mind, all about Antonio. Instead of asking them, she awkwardly offered Sofia something to drink.

Over a cup of tea, Sofia finally started talking. "I would have come earlier, but Antonio said you needed space."

Was that what he thought? Was that why he hadn't attempted to contact her?

"He also said you're healed completely."

"I…am." Physically, at least. "Antonio is a virtuoso. Even my scars are negligible, and fading every day."

An exquisite smile adorned the woman's gorgeous face, which now Lili could see was an older, feminine version of Antonio's. "His scars are fading, too. He's been letting me and his siblings closer, and it's been…indescribable. I always felt my baby had survived, had grown strong and special, but Antonio surpasses my every fantasy."

As he surpassed Lili's. So much so it was why she'd always felt she couldn't possibly deserve his love.

Sofia went on. "He told me you asked him to give me a chance. So I owe you the happiness of having my son back." Her smile faded as she continued. "But he abhors many members of the family for being of the same school of thought that led my parents to deprive me of him, and toss him into the nightmarish fate he still won't tell me about. These people owe you their *lives*, since you're the one who stayed his hand."

She'd had that much influence on him? Or had he just considered none worth the trouble of revenge?

Whatever the reason, she took joy in knowing that he was letting go of his bitterness and rage, letting his family heal him, accepting the love he deserved. If her role in his life had been to get him to this point, it was enough for her. She wanted him happy, even if she'd never be again.

Sofia reached for one of her hands. "But I'm really here to express how sorry I am for everything that happened since I insisted you visit me when my house was such a mess. Antonio explained why overhearing us upset you so much, but he said nothing further. I feel so guilty."

Lili put her other hand on top of hers. "Listen, Sofia, the renovation was barricaded, and I stupidly barged inside it. I was an idiot to overreact and run away in the first place. You have nothing to feel guilty about."

Tears glittered in the woman's eyes. "Even so, I felt terrible, and so helpless watching everything come apart. Your wedding…"

Unable to hear another word about their aborted wedding, she interrupted Sofia. "That's another thing that was all my doing. But I'm only happy that I brought you and Antonio back together."

"If only I could do the same." Sofia hugged her. "I would have loved to have you as a daughter-in-law."

Stunned by the woman's display of affection, distressed that her words meant Sofia thought a reunion with Antonio wasn't in the cards, she numbly hugged her back. "I would have loved to have you as a mother-in-law, too."

From then on and until Sofia left, they diverted the conversation to less stressful areas. When she took her leave Sofia made Lili promise to keep in touch.

As she closed the door behind her, Lili felt a new friend had entered her life. But what would that matter if she'd couldn't bear having her in it, if she only reminded her she'd lost Antonio?

Would her very life matter if she had?

And she could no longer bear not knowing.

She had to let *him* tell her. If there was still a chance, or if she should just surrender to despair.

The decision to approach Antonio was easier made than executed. All morning, fear held her back. Uncertainty, which she'd always been unable to handle, was now what kept her going. Because part of uncertainty was hope. If she killed the hope that she had a chance with Antonio, her life wouldn't be worth living.

But she not only couldn't go on not knowing for sure either way, but something terrible roiled inside her, prodding her to seek him out today. Right *now*. It wasn't the usual longing that gnawed at her. It was something ferocious that demanded action.

Just as she was about to leave the house to go to his medical center where she knew he was every day, her cell phone vibrated.

It was a number she didn't know.

Heart hammering, hoping against hope that it was him, she answered. The deep, dark voice that poured into her ear almost had her pile in a heap on the ground.

Because it wasn't Antonio.

It took her a second to recognize the voice. Jakob Wolff.

"Hello, Lili, it's Jakob. I have Ivan with me and we were wondering if you could see us."

Trembling with worry, she croaked, "Of course. When and where?"

"Right now. We're parked right outside."

"Oh. Oh! Please, come right in."

Tripping in her haste, she rushed to the door, opening it in time to see the two men step out of an imposing Rolls Royce. Breath bated, she watched these two who were an intimate part of Antonio's life walk up to her door.

Inviting them in, leading them where she'd had Sofia just yesterday, Lili and Ivan were soon immersed in their first face-to-face meeting. He seemed as curious about her as she was about him. Until recently, Ivan had been the closest person in the world to Antonio. If they'd gone through with the wedding, Ivan would have been his best man, would have become the brother she never had.

Suddenly Jakob sat forward, making Lili aware of his presence again, and of his impatience. "We're not here for chitchat."

Ivan sighed, nodded, got a dossier out of his briefcase, handed it to her. "Indeed. We're here to give you this."

Confusion deepening, she took it from him, and at his prodding, opened it and read.

With each line, each page, her shock deepened.

These were legal documents. Written in extensive, meticulous terms. Turning over Antonio's R & D empire to her.

When she finally raised flabbergasted eyes to them, Jakob's lips curled in disgusted disapproval. "Antonio believes you're better equipped to benefit the world with what he's built. He also believes you'd probably want to segregate it from Black Castle and become your own independent business, which he believes would be best for you and for your nonprofit policies and pursuits."

"If you're wondering what he'd do instead," Ivan said, watching her closely as if to document her reaction, "he'll turn full-time to what he's best at. Surgery. But he says he'll now emulate you, direct his skills and resources to nonprofit work. But as a surgeon, that would take him into the field of humanitarian work. He's already organized his first mission."

Lili stared from one man to the other, as if they'd suddenly laugh and tell her it was all an elaborate joke.

But from their grimness and their clear dismay at their brother's bequest, and mostly from the wording in those papers, which she knew was Antonio's, this was real.

"Needless to say," Ivan said, "we are extremely disturbed by his decision. We know no one could ever replace him, but since it's you, the others have empowered us to extend you an offer. We will accommodate anything you wish, if you agree to keep the division part of our joint business."

She could only stare at them, totally numb.

Jakob added, "He also said you'd have qualms on account of having no financial or management skills, but he assures you everything will be run by his deputies, while you orchestrate the scientific direction of the organization. He himself will always be available to you as a consultant whenever you wish."

And it was as if a dam burst inside her, making her blurt out, "Is he insane?"

Ivan nodded with another sigh. "Bonkers."

"It gets worse." Jakob produced another file from his own briefcase. "These are the deeds to his mansion in LA, his penthouse in New York City, his best jet, and assorted assets and holdings with a collective net worth I couldn't stomach registering."

She felt as if she'd been caught in an explosion, and the shock waves were widening, tearing down everything.

All she could finally manage was a whisper. "I—I don't get it."

"Don't you?" Jakob tilted his head, a contemptuous edge creeping into his steel-hued gaze, making him look pretty sinister. "From where I'm sitting, you seem to have gotten everything you could have wanted and way more."

She shook her head, shell-shocked. "I only want him."

"Now *that's* priceless." Jakob scoffed. "You dare say that, when you put the man through a hell far worse than all his ordeals combined?"

Ivan frowned. "Jakob's right on this one. According to Antonio you had every right to punish him, but I kept hoping you'd stop your punishment before you finished him. When you went past even that, I wondered what kind of succubus could do that to him. Then I saw you and I don't get it. You're filled with marshmallows and rainbows. How could you do this to him?"

"I didn't do anything," she cried out. "How could I punish him when I thought what he felt for me was...*nothing* like what I felt for him? When he left me alone after he discharged me, and I thought he'd realized he was better off without me, as I always thought he would be?"

Ivan's eyes narrowed before they shot wide. "That's it. That's my answer. You're really *that* insecure, aren't you?"

A shudder of misery shook her. "Only when it comes to him."

Ivan huffed mirthlessly. "Then, boy, are you two even. He's totally, explosively, inventively irrational when it comes to you, too. The man has been punishing himself for hurting you far more brutally than any of our abusers ever did."

"The only thing that hurt me was thinking he didn't... didn't..."

"Didn't love you?" Ivan supplied for her. "If he loved you any more he'd be downright dangerous. As it is, I think he is, very much so, to himself. All this…" Ivan flicked a hand at all the paperwork. "Signing his life away to you? Going to put bodies back together in the most dangerous war zone he could find? He might not be doing it consciously, but I know him. He's given up on you, and he can't face life without you, so like a missile on its last burst of fuel, he's trying to go out with a bang."

The horror of Ivan's analysis and prophecy froze the blood in her arteries.

Then she exploded, pouncing on the two men, shoving the folders at them and dragging them up. "You have to stop him!"

Jakob's gaze became contemptuous. "You think we didn't try? After the number you did on him, he's been like an automaton with no course-correction function left."

Anger broke through her distress. She grabbed Jakob's arm, shaking him. "Aren't all of you all-powerful? *Do* something!"

Still probing her, Jakob remained unperturbed by her agitation. "Antonio instructed us to give you all this after he left for his mission."

The world spun, made her stagger back. "He—he already left?"

Jakob steadied her, his gaze no longer accusing. "Not exactly, but that was another instruction. Not to tell you when he left or where he went."

Ivan took her arm, turned her to him. "And that's actually why we're here now. To tell you he's leaving tonight. Because we're not the ones who're all-powerful here. You are. The only one who can stop him is you."

Lili believed Ivan and Jakob would never talk to her again.

Not after she'd blasted them for wasting all that time

---

testing her and not telling her about Antonio's plans right away.

She'd also drafted them for a ride to his mansion, where they said he'd be, packing and emptying it for her possession. On the way, with Antonio's phone shut off, going mad thinking she'd be too late, she'd piled more and more invective on their sullen, silent heads.

Now they both turned to glare at her as she spilled out of the car at Antonio's door.

Before they drove off in a shower of gravel, Jakob shouted from his window, "You broke him, now you fix him."

Lili rushed to the front door. Climbing steps was still awkward for her, but she took them two at a time.

She entered the mansion to total silence, and dread almost chomped her in half. Was she too late? She'd failed to intercept him before he disappeared out of reach, maybe forever?

Terror mushroomed out of her on a scream. *"Antonio!"*

Footsteps exploded from the direction of the bedroom, which had been theirs once. They thundered before abruptly stopping. And then Antonio appeared across the great room.

He froze, just like she did.

But even across the distance his eyes told her everything, explained everything, put to rest everything that had been driving her insane.

He did share her heartache and misery, felt her same desperation and pain. But his agony seemed to have broken him. Her invulnerable Antonio. She'd done this to him.

Would he leave still because she'd hurt him beyond repair?

Suffocating with dread, all she could say was, "I love you. Please forgive me. Don't go." Then everything turned black.

* * *

"Liliana!"

Antonio exploded into a run and caught her before she hit the ground in a dead faint. After a frenzied exam proved she was physically fine, he rushed her to his bed. The bed he hadn't come near since she'd left him.

Though he knew from his obsessive follow-up of her condition that she was perfectly healed, she looked so spent and fragile. Just like he'd felt...until he'd heard her screaming his name, seen her standing there, her eyes open to him again, showing him into the depths of her soul. Until she'd said she loved him and asked him not to go.

Holding her made him feel as if the heart that had been ripped out of his body was restored. Feeling her warm and whole and *there*, he felt that the life that had oozed out of him every second since he'd lost her was returning. She was here to revive him, to give him another lease on life.

She came to with a gasp, her eyes frantic before she saw him. Then she came apart, clinging to him, a quaking, weeping mass.

Her sobs tore him up inside. "Don't go, please. Don't leave me. Don't leave me anything of yours. I want you, only ever you...please..."

His lips silenced her agony, his tears mingling with hers. "And I want only you. I wanted to leave everything behind when I thought you could no longer want me back."

She wrenched at his neck, his chest with trembling lips, soaking his flesh with her tears, covering it with the worship he'd withered without. "I'll stop wanting you when I stop breathing. Probably not even then."

Before he succumbed to the need to reclaim her, he had to know one thing for sure.

He rose above her, holding her precious face in his trembling hands. "Do you forgive me, *mi amore*? *Really* forgive me, for how I once planned to use you? I don't want the least doubt or bitterness lurking in your heart. That's what you said that day I let you go—that's why I couldn't persist anymore. I felt I could overcome your pain, but I would never erase your mistrust. And I couldn't do that to you. So do you really believe that I loved you from the beginning, and that I did change for you?"

She burst out in another weeping jag, dragging him down to her and deluging him with kisses and tears. "I believe you. I'll always believe you."

After the storm had abated, she drew back to look at him with such earnestness. "But I want you to promise me that if you ever feel any differently, you will tell me. You must never hide anything from me again, whether you're afraid it would hurt me, or know for sure it would."

"I take it this is a two-way street? If you ever stop feeling the same as you do right now, you'll tell me?"

"Since I'll never stop loving you, the only thing I'll confess is that I'm loving you more."

"But if for some unimaginable reason you stop loving me?"

She rose, her eyes telling him everything he needed to breathe again, to live again. "I'll always tell you the whole truth. You know I'm incapable of saying anything else."

"I know." His groan exorcised the last of his tension. Then he let her push him on his back, reveling in her beauty and honesty and openness, all the treasures he'd thought he would never be blessed with again, in the absoluteness of her love, which he'd thought he'd destroyed. "It's why I was in such despair. I knew you would never exaggerate to punish me, so I truly thought I'd lost you forever."

"I would have remained yours forever even if I never found my way back to you."

"And what good would that have done me?" he exclaimed.

She took his lips in a deep, devouring kiss before she pulled back, a grin lighting up her beauty. "I'd already found my way back to you. When your brothers arrived to give me your insane bequest and tell me of your crazy plans, I—"

He heaved up, his whole body tensing. "Those bastards! I'm going to strangle each and every one of them. I told them not to—" Then it hit him. "What am I saying? It's because they disobeyed me that you're here in my arms again."

"Actually, it isn't. That's what I was trying to say. I was coming to you when they came knocking." She looped her arms around his neck. "It seems I felt you were going to do something drastic, and I reached my limit at the same time you did."

"Even if you hadn't, and you decided much later to call me back, I would have come running."

"If I'd missed you, you would have come back to find your brothers roasted." At his incomprehension, she grinned sheepishly. "They put me through their elaborate tests to determine if I'd been manipulating you into giving me what you left me. It almost made me too late to stop you. If it had, I would have turned into a fire-breathing dragon."

A guffaw escaped him, the world suddenly bright and limitless again. "That must have been Jakob and Ivan. No other brother who got his wife's seal of approval on you would have *dared* suspect you of any ulterior motives."

"Yeah, it was Starsky and Hutch." As another laugh burst out of him, she clung to him again, her shudder shaking through him. "Promise me that whatever humanitarian missions you undertake won't be in areas of active conflict. If you don't want to kill me with worry."

Taking her down, he covered her, pressed into her, as

if he wanted to absorb her into his being. "I'd never put myself in harm's way when you need me."

Her fingers convulsed in his hair as she pulled his head up, her eyes fierce with conviction. "The whole world needs you, alive and well and being the irreplaceable force for good that you are. And this brings me to your bequest. All I'll ever need from you is your heart, your trust, your appreciation. But only you can direct everything you've built and achieved."

"You do have a better scientific mind than me."

"My mind and whatever else I have are at your service always. It will be an honor, a privilege and a pleasure to work with you in any capacity. But only you know how to bring everything together, to create and grow the best businesses that are beneficial to the world. You must take everything back." She suddenly chuckled, her golden eyes gleaming. "If you only saw your brothers imagining me filling your shoes, you wouldn't have had the heart to suggest it. Holmes and Watson were having little heart attacks at the very thought."

His laughter rang out with hers, until they were both almost in tears all over again.

Then merriment turned to passion, then to desperation and they were tearing each other's clothes off, competing to give more pleasure, to drag the other deeper into oblivion.

After repeated storms, full domination and surrender, Antonio rose above her and finally touched the places he'd avoided all night. Her faint scars. As he traced them, tears blinded him.

At her gasp, he raised his gaze, found her own eyes streaming again. She realized how he felt.

He still needed to put his feelings into words. "Those moments when your lifeblood bathed my hands as I struggled to stem it, when I was forced to cut into your flesh to save your precious life, when I felt you fighting me so you could let go... I'll never heal from them."

Hers sobs fractured her breath, her words. "I'm sorry, so sorry."

Wiping at his eyes, he smiled with everything in him. "Never be sorry for anything. Just like you made me a new man who has no rage or darkness, who can be ecstatically in love, who can be a son and a brother, you've probably absolved me from every sin I've ever committed. This punishment is enough to take care of all of them. I only wish you didn't have to get hurt so I'd be punished. It's a catch-22 really, since I can only be hurt through you."

Her dawning grin caught on another sob. "I hate being your Achilles' heel."

He hugged her again. "But I love having you as my only vulnerability. I can't live without you being everything to me. My strength and weakness, my joy and agony, my desire and dread."

"You're all that to me and everything else and it's... enormous."

Heart swelling with gratitude, he nodded sagely. "Humongous."

They shared another moment of total communion, before they laughed again. Their mirth caught fire again and they were again surrendering to the power of their bottomless passion and hunger.

Afterward she lay satiated in his arms, wondering what she'd ever done in her life to deserve him.

As if he'd heard her thoughts, he turned her face to him, his words sounding like an irrevocable pledge.

"The heart that grew inside me from the first moment I saw you is yours forever because you gave it life. You changed my perspective and priorities. You made me let go of my anger against my family even before I met them.

It's because of you that I gave them and myself a chance, why I have them back in my life now. You're the reason I *have* a life, not just a race for more achievements and acquisitions. You're the reason I want to live forever."

The tears that came so easily to her now flowed again, ones of bliss this time. "Maybe immortality should be my new research, then. I've been eyeing gene therapy for longevity for a while now."

"If anyone could find its secret, it's you." He gathered her tighter, his expression becoming adamant. "And it *is* you who's more qualified scientifically to run the research division, while I want to give back to the world now. And that's another reason I'm yours. Until I met you, I took what I thought life owed me, and I gave back only strategically, to increase my profits. But now that I've found you, now that you love me, the world has given me far more than I can ever deserve. Now I have to create balance, give back everything I can so that I can continue to deserve having the miracle of you and your love."

Drowning in his love, in relief and gratitude, she took hold of the hands that had given her her life back, took them to her lips as she gave him her own pledge.

"And I only want the privilege of sharing your exceptional journey. You have all of me—the heart that grew to love you, the body you awakened and owned and saved, the soul that became whole only when you healed it, and everything else that I am. They're all yours, my love. Now and forever."

* * * * *

MILLS & BOON®
Hardback – September 2016

ROMANCE

To Blackmail a Di Sione	Rachael Thomas
A Ring for Vincenzo's Heir	Jennie Lucas
Demetriou Demands His Child	Kate Hewitt
Trapped by Vialli's Vows	Chantelle Shaw
The Sheikh's Baby Scandal	Carol Marinelli
Defying the Billionaire's Command	Michelle Conder
The Secret Beneath the Veil	Dani Collins
The Mistress That Tamed De Santis	Natalie Anderson
Stepping into the Prince's World	Marion Lennox
Unveiling the Bridesmaid	Jessica Gilmore
The CEO's Surprise Family	Teresa Carpenter
The Billionaire from Her Past	Leah Ashton
A Daddy for Her Daughter	Tina Beckett
Reunited with His Runaway Bride	Robin Gianna
Rescued by Dr Rafe	Annie Claydon
Saved by the Single Dad	Annie Claydon
Sizzling Nights with Dr Off-Limits	Janice Lynn
Seven Nights with Her Ex	Louisa Heaton
The Boss's Baby Arrangement	Catherine Mann
Billionaire Boss, M.D.	Olivia Gates

0816 GEN STD HB

MILLS & BOON®
Large Print – September 2016

ROMANCE

Morelli's Mistress	Anne Mather
A Tycoon to Be Reckoned With	Julia James
Billionaire Without a Past	Carol Marinelli
The Shock Cassano Baby	Andie Brock
The Most Scandalous Ravensdale	Melanie Milburne
The Sheikh's Last Mistress	Rachael Thomas
Claiming the Royal Innocent	Jennifer Hayward
The Billionaire Who Saw Her Beauty	Rebecca Winters
In the Boss's Castle	Jessica Gilmore
One Week with the French Tycoon	Christy McKellen
Rafael's Contract Bride	Nina Milne

HISTORICAL

In Bed with the Duke	Annie Burrows
More Than a Lover	Ann Lethbridge
Playing the Duke's Mistress	Eliza Redgold
The Blacksmith's Wife	Elisabeth Hobbes
That Despicable Rogue	Virginia Heath

MEDICAL

The Socialite's Secret	Carol Marinelli
London's Most Eligible Doctor	Annie O'Neil
Saving Maddie's Baby	Marion Lennox
A Sheikh to Capture Her Heart	Meredith Webber
Breaking All Their Rules	Sue MacKay
One Life-Changing Night	Louisa Heaton

MILLS & BOON®
Hardback – October 2016

ROMANCE

The Return of the Di Sione Wife	Caitlin Crews
Baby of His Revenge	Jennie Lucas
The Spaniard's Pregnant Bride	Maisey Yates
A Cinderella for the Greek	Julia James
Married for the Tycoon's Empire	Abby Green
Indebted to Moreno	Kate Walker
A Deal with Alejandro	Maya Blake
Surrendering to the Italian's Command	Kim Lawrence
Surrendering to the Italian's Command	Kim Lawrence
A Mistletoe Kiss with the Boss	Susan Meier
A Countess for Christmas	Christy McKellen
Her Festive Baby Bombshell	Jennifer Faye
The Unexpected Holiday Gift	Sophie Pembroke
Waking Up to Dr Gorgeous	Emily Forbes
Swept Away by the Seductive Stranger	Amy Andrews
One Kiss in Tokyo...	Scarlet Wilson
The Courage to Love Her Army Doc	Karin Baine
Reawakened by the Surgeon's Touch	Jennifer Taylor
Second Chance with Lord Branscombe	Joanna Neil
The Pregnancy Proposition	Andrea Laurence
His Illegitimate Heir	Sarah M. Anderson

MILLS & BOON®
Large Print – October 2016

ROMANCE

Wallflower, Widow...Wife!	Ann Lethbridge
Bought for the Greek's Revenge	Lynne Graham
An Heir to Make a Marriage	Abby Green
The Greek's Nine-Month Redemption	Maisey Yates
Expecting a Royal Scandal	Caitlin Crews
Return of the Untamed Billionaire	Carol Marinelli
Signed Over to Santino	Maya Blake
Wedded, Bedded, Betrayed	Michelle Smart
The Greek's Nine-Month Surprise	Jennifer Faye
A Baby to Save Their Marriage	Scarlet Wilson
Stranded with Her Rescuer	Nikki Logan
Expecting the Fellani Heir	Lucy Gordon

HISTORICAL

The Many Sins of Cris de Feaux	Louise Allen
Scandal at the Midsummer Ball	Marguerite Kaye & Bronwyn Scott
Marriage Made in Hope	Sophia James
The Highland Laird's Bride	Nicole Locke
An Unsuitable Duchess	Laurie Benson

MEDICAL

Seduced by the Heart Surgeon	Carol Marinelli
Falling for the Single Dad	Emily Forbes
The Fling That Changed Everything	Alison Roberts
A Child to Open Their Hearts	Marion Lennox
The Greek Doctor's Secret Son	Jennifer Taylor
Caught in a Storm of Passion	Lucy Ryder

MILLS & BOON®

Why shop at millsandboon.co.uk?

Each year, thousands of romance readers find their perfect read at millsandboon.co.uk. That's because we're passionate about bringing you the very best romantic fiction. Here are some of the advantages of shopping at www.millsandboon.co.uk:

* **Get new books first**—you'll be able to buy your favourite books one month before they hit the shops

* **Get exclusive discounts**—you'll also be able to buy our specially created monthly collections, with up to 50% off the RRP

* **Find your favourite authors**—latest news, interviews and new releases for all your favourite authors and series on our website, plus ideas for what to try next

* **Join in**—once you've bought your favourite books, don't forget to register with us to rate, review and join in the discussions

Visit **www.millsandboon.co.uk**
for all this and more today!